Irish Eyes

A *Timeless* American Historical Romance: Book 2

By

Suzanne Rudd Hamilton

HHH Press

This is a work of fiction. Names, characters, places, and incidents are products of the author's imagination or are used fictitiously. Any resemblance to actual events or locales or persons, living or dead, is entirely coincidental.

Irish Eyes: Copyright © 2022 by Suzanne Rudd Hamilton

All rights reserved. Except as permitted under U.S. Copyright Act of 1976, no part of this book may be reproduced, stored in a retrievable system, or transmitted by any means without written permission from the author.

ISBN: 9798835249305

Imprint: HHH Press

Suzanne Rudd Hamilton

Chapter One

Spring 1933

Davey ventured up the dark stairs to his grandmother Maggie's attic. A small beam of daylight through the lone window showed dust particles dancing like stars, shining a beacon on some old wooden boxes.

To some it was an old dusty den of forgotten junk, but to Davey, the attic was an adventure land of untold tales yet to be discovered. The bicycles hanging from the ceiling turned the gears of his greatest inventions, the dozen-odd chairs were lined up to seat the jury of his client's murder trial and the clothesline of drying flowers was a forest of vines he had to slash to save the princess from the horrible dragon.

Since he was a small boy, this was his playground on those cold Chicago days when he visited his grandmother's brick bungalow. Indoor imagination was the only outing possible.

The chill in the early spring air prompted inside activities and a feast for imagination. Luckily, the yellow-tinted sunrays spotlighted the wooden boxes for a new quest. Maybe they could be a throne for the new King

David to dispense wisdom. Or a platform for a circus performer to try death-defying feats of amazing skill.

Davey opened the boxes to see what treasures lay within. He quickly dug through them to find dried flowers, some lace, old pins that read "Vote for Women" and "Together We Stand," some faded sashes and ribbons, gloves and a straw hat.

"Girl stuff," Davey said wrinkling his nose, taking the straw hat and closed the box.

In another box he found a vest, picture scrapbook and old worn pamphlets and postcards with drawings of lions, buildings, snakes and a big Ferris Wheel. He took the vest and leafed through the illustrations.

"That's it," he said jumped up with enthusiasm, putting on the hat and vest and picking up a nearby cane.

"Step right up, ladies and gentlemen, to see the ferocious lions from Africa and slithering snakes from the Far East in the greatest show on earth, Davey's Carnival," he shouted, imitating a carnival barker.

The sound of applause coming up the stairs interrupted him when his grandmother appeared, clapping and laughing.

"It sounds grand. I'll take one ticket, young sir," Maggie smiled at her creative grandson.

Davey was taken aback by her unexpected arrival but stayed in character.

"Ma'am are you ready to see the strangest and most wonderful things in the universe?" he asked.

"As I stand here before ya, I can't say as I'd be wondering about anything else," she said with her thick Irish brough.

Davey laughed, put down the cane and took off the hat, showing his grandmother the treasures he found.

"Gran, I was looking through these boxes and saw some papers with drawings of lions and snakes and a Ferris Wheel. Did you really see those things at this fair?" he asked.

Maggie picked up the straw hat and laughed. "This old thing just never seems to go out of style."

She sat in an old chair beside him and opened the wooden boxes, slowly sifting through the baubles and trinkets of memories within.

"Aye. These old green eyes seen many and done a few. Me mother always said don't resent growing old, as many are denied the privilege. I'm glad for me years, but me boy, these momentos are the things that bring memories back to life. The silky feel of an old glove. The lasting smell of dried heather and lavender. Your grandpop loved to bring me flowers. A picture or postcard left behind long ago. It all shows where you been and makes what you are." She smiled as she lingered on each object.

"Gran, are there any pictures of Ireland? I like when you tell me about the green grass and the sea breezes." Davey sat at her feet, eagerly looking up at her.

Maggie looked through the boxes and picked up a small picture scrapbook and showed it to him.

"Well, here is the house we lived in. Windermere. It was a beautiful place with acres of green grass all around. You can't see the green here, but that's why it's called the Emerald Isle, you know," she said as she pointed to the washed-out black-and-white photographs.

"And there's me mother and here's one of me and Carrie when we were wee ones," she said pensively, staring at the pictures. "It was so long ago. Like another lifetime."

Summer 1875

Caroline Stevens and Maggie Donnelly were the best of friends. They grew up together on Windermere, Caroline's family home on hundreds of sprawling green acres in County Donegal. Mr. Stevens, Caroline's father, was a country lawyer who came from money.

Windermere was a typical country manor house of the well-to-do, clad in sleek white stone with just enough ivy positioned to make it look respectable.

Thanks to Mrs. Stevens, the décor was stylish and elegant, given that she wished to move into higher circles.

But it was a working farm with farm hands, sheep, horses, fields of crops and green rolling hills.

The house was stately with enough room to keep the family and a small group of servants inside with a coach house for the farm hands. And Maggie's mother Katherine was the housekeeper, running the small household and tirelessly tending to every need of the family and the home.

As they were both only children and the same age, Caroline and Maggie grew up side by side, like sisters. Caroline—or Carrie, as Maggie called her—was petite with alabaster skin, bright blue eyes and long corn-blonde hair, while Maggie had curly red hair and freckles with piercing green eyes. No one would mistake them for actual sisters.

They romped through the amber and verdant rolling fields endlessly playing each day until exhaustion or the setting sun took hold.

Maggie always protected Caroline from trouble. If there was a pond to cross or fence to jump, Maggie would go first and find a way to keep Caroline from danger or mess. Caroline's mother liked proper little girls to stay tidy and ladylike.

As little babes, they played with dolls Maggie's mother made and a tea set Caroline's mother bought. When Maggie honed her seamstress skills, she created pretty lace doilies and fancy dresses for the new porcelain-faced dolls Caroline begged her mother to buy.

The houseman, Aaron, gave them lessons in numbers and reading for a few hours each day and Caroline's mother read the Bible to them, but the rest of each day was theirs to imagine, laugh and play carefree.

When they were together, the lines between mistress and servant were bare. They were just two little girls.

One day, while running in the forest on the perimeter of the family's acreage, they found two strange trees off the beaten path where no one could see. They were an odd configuration of two trees a few feet apart that grew together, with their branches of foliage intertwined into a luscious canopy.

As soon as the girls found it, they decided that the branches improbably tangled together were made just for them. It was a special place they could hide away, giggle and tell secrets. Their own private area, where against all logic, the two trees joined to create a wondrous and lovely leafed crown—just like their friendship.

They called it their craobh rún—secret tree fort—and spent many days sitting under the shady leaves, playing games and singing songs. Whittling down branches to a fine point, they scrawled their names in the tree bark to mark it as theirs.

"We dub thee Caroline and Maggie's craobh rún for now and forever," young Caroline said, carving her name into one tree.

"Now it's ours for good," young Maggie said, etching her name in the other tree.

Sometimes they'd sneak out to look at the stars before they lay their heads down at harboo. Lying beneath the tree, they'd draw pictures in the heavens with their fingers, dreaming and singing a silly rhyme they concocted.

Wish, wish, shining star, make us be who we are, and if ye take us far from ours, keep us forever Anam Cara.

Over time, their starry canopy became a blank canvas to craft elaborate stories of the images they saw in the stars—why they were there or what they were doing. Caroline was particularly talented at creating narratives of the celestial inhabitants and their lives.

Maggie admired her great gift of imagination and tongue for tales, thinking she was blessed with a bit of the blarney in her and maybe her parents had her kiss the blarney stone more than once when she was a wee babe.

Years went by and the girls grew older. They took fewer book lessons and started to learn their trades.

Maggie continued perfecting her seamstress skills and learning domestic skills beside her mother. Caroline's mother taught her dancing, piano and all the talents and proficiencies necessary to be the lady of the house one day.

Although they spent less time together, they escaped for a few hours to ride horses and chitchat at their secret place, marking drawings and words in the bark. It looked like an album of their relationship from babes to girls to adults.

Even when their days were full of more grown-up endeavors, they would meet at night to discuss their daily adventures and sit out and watch the stars shine in the night sky.

"Mother goes on for days about correct posture, walking, and the right things to wear, say and do to attract and keep the right husband," Caroline sighed and lay down on the grass. "I've had my fill of it."

"I guess I can count myself blessed by a clover. Ma's a grand teacher," Maggie said. "Even when I get me ire up because I can't do something, she's patient as a saint. She tells me to count to three and breathe. She says me green eyes always give me away and me temper will get me in hot water someday."

"I feel like I'm the prized pig getting shined up and dressed in a big bow to earn a blue ribbon, just to get sold to the butcher for dinner," Caroline explained in frustration.

"Seems like finding a man is a lot of trouble. Me mother lived this long without a man and she's happy I'm not sure I'll be wanting one either," Maggie said.

"Lucky you—I don't have a choice," Caroline said, pulling grass and throwing it wildly into the air.

"Don't worry. It'll be a while before your ma and pa start making matches for ya," Maggie assured her.

Caroline sat up with a quick jolt. "No, it's now. Me ma, I mean my mother, is asking around for the right man. Before you know it, I'll be married off and be forced to leave my home… and you."

Maggie took her hand. "Well, that's that then. Don't fret, I'll just make meself part of the deal. Where you go, I go."

"You would do that for me?" Caroline gasped and smiled, holding Maggie's hand tightly.

"I'll always be with ya," Maggie grinned. "As me mother says, rust never grows on the hinges of good friendships."

But walking different paths, their divide widened. Maggie's growing household duties left her little time. And for Caroline, her duty to make herself available and desirable for suitable husbands became all consuming.

Caroline's mother vigorously made inquiries of nearby households to find the best mate for her pretty, well-brought-up daughter.

For weeks, then months, Caroline's mother dragged her around and introduced her to every society mother in the county. She finagled invitations to the best parties and dances and marketed her daughter to the mothers while sipping tea. Caroline smiled sweetly, sipped tea quietly and looked pretty for all the mothers, like shoppers looking at window dressing.

"There's my daughter, Caroline; not only is she beautiful but she takes lessons every day on etiquette and running a household," her mother bragged. "She'll be a fine wife for any man who wants to get ahead."

After many afternoons feeling like a dress in the window waiting for someone to buy her, Caroline confided her sorrows to Maggie in their craobh rún.

"Mother never stops. I constantly feel like I'm being inspected by the mothers. And the sons look a bucket of snots and act the fool eejit," Caroline said, plopping down on the grass.

"Me mother says there is only one thing worse than being talked about, and that is not being talked about. There's not one friendly lad?" Maggie asked.

"No. Aye. I don't know," she said, frustrated, while pulling grass and throwing it in the air.

"Since I was a girl, I dreamed of marrying a wonderful and handsome man who would be sweet to me and we'd have lots of babes and live happily ever after. But I don't have a choice. My mother just wants to find me a man from a fine and wealthy family. Nothing else matters."

Caroline laid back on the grass in a huff.

"Ya have to believe that he's out there, and when ya find him, put your grandest smile on, grab him with both hands and don't let go." Maggie started drawing on the tree. "But if ya find some frogs along the way, we'll just have to stick them on the lily pad and wave goodbye."

They both laughed and Caroline got up and followed Maggie, drawing frogs into the tree.

A month later, Caroline's mother received an invitation to the Donegal Hall annual ball, the grandest party of the year.

She immediately started Katherine and Maggie working on the perfect ballgown for Caroline. Sapphire blue satin with matching toile and homemade Irish lace would create a stunning dress to complement Caroline's blonde hair and accentuate her blue eyes.

Maggie used all her stitching skills to craft a magnificent dress for her friend. She made a bodice of the satin and intertwined ribbon in the lace sewn into the sheer sleeves and a wide multi-layered flowing toile skirt with satin underneath.

"This is beautiful my girl," Katherine said, marveling at the dress. "Everything is so intricate. You're ready to fly. I've nothing left to teach ye."

Caroline's eyes widened when she saw the dress.

"It's fit for a fairy-tale princess," she smiled. She held the dress up to her chin and twirled around with it, then hugged Maggie.

"I can't believe I get to wear this. You know me so well."

"I just hope it gets ya a perfect man of your dreams." Maggie smiled, pleased her friend loved the dress.

"I will be the most enviable girl at the ball. There's no stopping me now," Caroline glowed.

Chapter Two

Summer 1885

The ball was held at the home of the Donegal family, the richest family in County Donegal and the aristocracy of the area. Donegal Hall was a rebirthed sixteenth-century castle, renovated by the Lady Moira, the dowager countess of Donegal to represent the finest décor of the day.

The stately castle stood three stories of gleaming white stone with square turret towers on all four corners. A stone stairway led the way to the front entrance of two enormous wooden doors, which were swung wide open to welcome the guests.

Although there were balls and parties throughout the season, the dowager countess of Donegal held the main gala to debut all the proper young lasses to meet prospective husbands from the best families in Ireland. As part of the founding family of Donegal, she felt it was her duty to provide the breeding ground to direct the next generation of Irish elite.

And she paid particular attention to every detail of the event, from the music and the food to the splendid surroundings, sparing no expense.

After presenting her invitation to one footman, while another removed her cloak, Caroline gaped in awe at the sculpted designs above her heads and a series of tall flying buttresses cloistered in the entryway, leading passage to the grand ballroom.

The ballroom was the grandest in Ireland. Sparkling chandeliers twinkled light on the shimmering twenty-foot white plaster walls, dressed with intricate gold leaf accenting the diamond-shaped designs. Beautiful frescos painted in the middle diamond on each wall depicted genteel Irish country landscapes and gardens, while a magnificent trompe-l'œil painting in the middle of the wooden barrel-vault ceiling portrayed cherubs dancing in the fluffy clouds of a blue sky.

An endless table of fine food and drink lined one wall of the room, leaving plenty of space for dancing and conversations.

Always following correct form, the countess insisted all the girls were presented by herself or her two sisters to any young gentleman. She provided them with completed dance cards when they arrived to match candidates she deemed suitable for each girl. Lady Moira considered herself the finest matchmaker on the isle.

Caroline flushed and glowed with nervous energy and awe at the auspicious atmosphere. She was both excited and petrified at the prospect of meeting her Prince Charming, but her lack of experience around men made her unsure, her feet were firmly planted on the floor and her thoughts and words escaped from her head.

She stood there in silence against the wall, gazing at all the people but unable to move. Until a petite woman with a giant gold bird feather on her head approached her, towing a short uneasy young man.

"Now, Caroline Stevens, do you think you can hide in a painting if you stand there still as a statue?" she asked with an awkward chuckle. "May I introduce you to my son, Finley? He is your first dance partner."

Caroline smiled timidly and bowed her head slightly at the introduction. As the music began, Finley took her hand and led her onto the dance floor.

She was a good dancer, as her mother taught her all the proper dances. She and Maggie had practiced endlessly, with Maggie always pretending to be the boy.

Caroline glided along to the music, but Finley only briefly smiled at her while paying attention to a tall girl with long chestnut hair on the other side of the room.

Since this was her first season, Caroline was not adept at the elaborate game of cat and mouse played at these balls, with young lads and lasses jockeying for position and keeping tabs on their favorites. Needless to say, the ball matrons' matchmaking didn't always align with the desires of their adolescent subjects.

When the dance ended, Caroline curtsied to her partner and he presented her to the next partner, as it went on all night. Some of the boys were so tall, she had to stand on her tiptoes for her petite frame to compete. The shorter ones were easier to dance with and seemed to be relieved at her diminutive five-foot height, so they could unusually command the vertical space over her.

There was little talking, just polite quips about the party, the music and the food. Many of the boys seemed stilted or preoccupied and uninterested in meeting eyes. But Caroline was unaffected. It was her first party and her mind was spinning with all the color, sound and life of the lively event.

Every half-hour or so, the band stopped for a brief pause and everyone assembled around the table for food and drink, gathering in small clusters. While she recognized one or two people from the ladies' teas, she didn't know anyone well enough to approach their closed cliques, so Caroline once again found a spot in front of a fresco. She was too nervous to eat or drink, so she just stood and observed the activity in the room. It was unlike anything she ever saw.

Girls were standing together in groups gossiping and giggling and boys were bunched watching the girls. It was like a game. One or two girls would purposely walk past a group of boys and throw them a look or a smile. And usually one boy would walk up to a group of girls. If they noticed a relative or close friend of the family, they would start a conversation with them, awaiting introduction to the rest of the girls.

Sometimes, after introductions were made, a boy and girl will peel off and begin talking to each other.

After witnessing this a few times, Caroline decided the girls were scouting elicit interest from the boys. And the more confident boys would try to gain entry and introduction into the circle, so he could begin talking to a girl he favored. Luckily there always seemed to be a sister, cousin or a close family friend to approach and facilitate the presentation.

It seemed a silly ritual, but she longed to be involved. Unfortunately, as she was from the country, without relatives and new on the scene, Caroline had no one but the matrons to help her.

"Quite the routine this is, wouldn't you say?" asked a man suddenly standing next to Caroline, giving her a fright. She was so entranced in the ceremony of courtships going on that she neither heard nor saw him. She peeped a little sound from the scare.

"I didn't mean to make you cheep like a little chick," he laughed. "Did I frighten you?"

Caroline blushed with embarrassment, looking down to avoid his glance.

"My apologies, sir, I did not see you approach," she said quietly.

"No need. I often like to watch the absurdity of this mating game. You are clever to remain still so someone misjudges you for part of the painting—then you can remain invisible and unengaged. Quite reasonable of you," he said while eating a plate of food.

At first, Caroline was mortified that again she was mistaken for trying to blend into a painting, but upon consideration she realized what she was doing. In her camouflage perch, she could observe in peace and go completely unnoticed. And now that she had an opportunity to participate, she was at a loss as to what to say or do. All she could get out was a brief and inaudible giggle in response.

"You're like a pretty little bird—what's your name?" he asked.

"Caroline Stevens," she said meekly, raising her head to meet his gaze. "This is my first ball."

She nearly gasped as she first looked upon his tall handsome stature with bright hazel eyes, wavy chestnut brown hair and a chiseled square jaw with a whimsical cleft in the chin.

"I thought you were a novice," he said confidently, chuckling. "Be careful in the shark-infested waters."

And he left as quickly as he came. Caroline's head was in a swirl of emotions, from awkwardness to curiosity to confusion. She could barely remember the exchange, but she couldn't forget his face. As she stood there alone again, her eyes followed him around the room as he went back to the banquet table and then walked around nodding to people, but barely stopping to talk to anyone.

She sighed as she watched his every move. He was tall and slender, gliding across the room as if his feet didn't touch the ground. His brown curly hair waved across his forehead on one side, revealing his sideways smile and hazel eyes.

When the music began again, Caroline was interrupted from her trance.

"Miss Caroline Stevens, I presume. I am Mrs. Murphy. This is my son Derrin Murphy and this is your dance," she said.

He led her around the dance floor, followed by several other couples who began dancing after the break.

And then there was another partner and another. Caroline was so preoccupied with her mystery man, she barely remembered anyone she danced with, until she was formally introduced to him, Mr. Bryne Donegal.

The name of the host hardly permeated her cloud bubble thoughts until she raised her head to acknowledge the tall stranger and locked eyes with him, smiling down at her.

"Guess now we're a match, little bird," he laughed and took her hand.

Her hand vibrated in shock waves flowing through her whole body right to her toes at his mere touch on her fingertips. As the song began, she couldn't hear the music or see anyone else, as her eyes, ears, and all her senses were enthralled by his presence. He smiled at her and she returned his glance, unconsciously grinning in silence as he guided them both across the dance floor.

She was like a rag doll moving to his every ebb, so mesmerized that she hardly felt her feet tap the floor. Caroline was blissfully floating on a cloud of amorous until he abruptly stopped.

"Sir, this is my dance," came the echo of a voice.

"I think Miss Stevens would prefer my company," Bryne chuckled. He brushed off the young man as the music resumed and they danced again.

Caroline was speechless and hopelessly captivated. She felt as if she had left her body; she had no control of any of her functions.

But she didn't care. For the rest of the night, she remained locked in his dance frame with her hand in his, gleefully circling in her dream bubble.

"Little bird… are you there, little bird?" he asked, teasing her.

Caroline startled, awakening from her daze while gazing up, smiling at him.

"Good. I don't know where you went, but it must be lovely from the look on your face," he smiled.

Caroline was screaming at herself to say something. Anything. So he would know how she felt.

"It was simply wonderful to dance with you," she said softly and bowed her head. He grinned and bowed to her, then left.

The party was over and she was in heaven.

Somehow, she retrieved her cloak, exited the castle, and got into her carriage, but she remembered nothing as her driver took her home.

"Carrie—Carrie girl, are ya ailing? Should I call your mother?" Maggie asked, helping her out of the carriage.

Caroline snapped out of her blissful mind fog when she heard Maggie's voice.

"Oh, Maggie, it was so wonderful. I'm walking on air." She twirled her cloak around in a circle.

Maggie laughed and brought her into the house. Caroline regaled her with every detail of the night as Maggie helped her change. She unwrapped every piece of the event like a shiny bauble, leaving nothing untold. The castle, the ballroom, the food, the people and her prince charming, Bryne.

Caroline excitedly spun the minute-by-minute yarn, keeping Maggie in breathless anticipation of each and every aspect of the ball. Caroline's storytelling prowess swept Maggie in the swirl of romantic adventure. After she was through, they both let out a deep relaxing sigh at the final word.

"I'm in love, Maggie. I don't exactly know what it is, but I know I want to feel that way for the rest of my life," she confided.

"Really? Already? It sounded marvelous, but this is your first ball. There will be so many more dances and boys," Maggie said.

"I would love to go to more parties, but there are no more boys for me, only Bryne," she beamed. "I'll think of him every moment I'm awake and dream of him every second of my slumber."

Suzanne Rudd Hamilton

     Maggie smiled as she left her friend in such a gleeful state. She went to bed in awe at the woven tale Caroline spun, wondering if she would ever experience anything that extraordinary.

Chapter Three

The next morning as the sun arose, a messenger came to the back door with a bouquet of beautiful canary buttercups, purple violets, and pink pillows of bog-rosemary with an envelope addressed to Miss Caroline Stevens.

Katherine arranged the flowers in a vase and gave it to Maggie for Caroline's room. And she took the envelope to Caroline's mother.

Maggie ran up the stairs so fast, she skipped a few steps, excited to give Caroline her first flowers.

"Carrie, Carrie—look, look!" she yelled to a sleepy Caroline. "These came for you!"

Caroline wiped the night sand from her eyes and quickly focused on the flowers.

"These are for me?" she screamed happily. "Are they from him?"

"I hardly know, but I expect so. Your mother has the card; it was addressed to Miss Caroline Stevens," Maggie said.

The girls sat on the bed admiring the beautiful flowers, mooning over the sweet gesture and so soon after the ball.

Their daydreaming was interrupted when Mrs. Stevens came in the door with the flower card in her hand.

"Maggie, leave us, please."

Maggie quickly left and closed the door. She was wrapped up in curiosity, but she knew Carrie would tell her all about it later at the tree.

"Seems like you made quite an impression at the ball," Mrs. Stevens said, smiling. "The flowers and card are from Mr. Bryne Donegal and his mother, the dowager countess, inviting us to call for tea tomorrow afternoon."

Caroline sighed glowing, as she told her mother about the ball and their encounter. Unlike her retelling to Maggie, she tailored a less fanciful version for her mother's ears about how beautiful the house was and how she met the wonderful Bryne.

"He's the one for me, Mother. The only one," she pined.

"I'm very pleased," Mrs. Stevens nodded. "The Donegals are a very wealthy family and titled. The cream of the crop. They could provide an excellent boost into society for us all and could help your father's business. Good job. I taught you well."

Caroline had her head so far into the stars fantasizing of her life with Bryne, she just smiled and nodded, not hearing a word her mother said.

For the rest of the day, she walked on stardust around the house, humming and bouncing around.

When Maggie got to the tree that day, Caroline had all the twigs and flowers lined up in a wedding processional.

"This is where I'll walk down the aisle. Now I want a big veil, enough to fill the whole aisle—one I would need several maids to carry behind me. You can do that, right? I think satin and lace would be wonderful. I know blue is traditional, but since Queen Victoria wore white, many brides have followed fashion. Do you think ivory or white would be better?" Caroline rattled on without taking a breath.

"He asked for your hand already?" Maggie shouted with eyes bulging in shock.

"No, but that is just a matter of time," she giggled. "We need to start planning."

Maggie's head was in a daze, confused by Caroline's rash leap from I just met him to I'm marrying him all in one day.

"Carrie, I'm dying—for the love of God, what was in the envelope?" Maggie pleaded.

"Oh, sorry. I'm so excited about the planning, I forgot to tell you. It was an invitation," Caroline said, preoccupied with arranging the twigs and flowers.

Maggie's face turned as red as her hair, bursting with curiosity.

"And may I ask, what was the invitation for and who from?"

Caroline started humming the Wedding March.

"Oh, it was from Bryne and his mother, inviting us for tea tomorrow afternoon."

"Begorrah," Maggie plopped down on the grass surprised. "Come to think of it, I think ivory would be nice."

※

Afternoon tea was a staple in Ireland for all, but in society circles, it was a mark of importance to be invited take tea at someone's house. The invitation wasn't merely to drink; it was an opportunity to see and be seen, but also a polite point of vetting for a prospective acquaintance to measure up.

Caroline and her mother primped for hours, toiling over each and every aspect of their wardrobe. The color, the hat, the type of dress, everything would be scrutinized to present them as either the right or wrong kind of people. Maggie helped Caroline and Katherine helped Mrs. Stevens dress and select the perfect outfits.

"I know this seems silly, but it's so important for his mother to like me," Caroline said nervously, buttoning and unfastening each button on her vest. "I'm so scared I will make a mistake and then that's it."

Maggie held Caroline's hands and smiled. "Just breathe, me girl, and let me take care of everything."

She fixed Caroline's blue vest over her yellow and white striped dress with and tied the cornflower blue ribbon around the scalloped collar. Then she pinned a blue-brimmed hat with a lace veil in the back, hanging over her blonde tresses.

"Ah, ya look beautiful. Just like a proper young lady," Maggie said.

"Oh Maggie, what would I do without you?" Caroline hugged her and put on her short white gloves. "You make everything look so lovely, just like you."

"Just remember, smile, be yourself and keep breathing. No one died from a tea," Maggie laughed.

Caroline and her mother climbed into the carriage. Her mother wore a smart canary waistcoat, pale yellow dress and white high collared lace blouse that complemented her tightly-bunned golden hair and blue eyes that were just like her daughter's. Thanks to Katherine and Maggie, the Stevens family attire was the envy of everyone they met. Their clothes were fashionable and well-tailored to look like they spent a fortune on their wardrobe. Even those who imported the latest Paris fashions admired their taste, vaulting them to higher levels than their fortune would deliver.

Mrs. Stevens was aghast at Donegal Hall when they arrived. Caroline stared in awe, even though she had already seen the estate, at the daylight beauty of the home when the footman ushered them into the solarium for tea.

"Welcome—please sit down," Countess Donegal said. "I'm so glad to make your acquaintance, Mrs. Stevens, and so happy to see you again, Miss Stevens."

The table was beautifully set with Irish lace cloth illuminated by the afternoon sunbeams gleaming into the glass solarium.

Dainty white china teacups with blue and yellow flowers and gold rims were placed in front of them with a plate tower of scones, cakes and jams in the middle. A shiny silver tea service set the table.

Countess Donegal dismissed her maid and picked up the milk in her own hand.

"Please allow me to be mother," she said as she gracefully poured milk into the small cups and took the silver teapot and poured the black tea.

"You must try the apple cakes," she said, smiling. "Cook makes them with apples from our own orchard."

Both ladies both took a cake and Caroline chose a biscuit, delicately spreading a small amount of jam on it, careful to avoid getting any jam on her pristine white gloves. Her mother's mountains of etiquette lessons paid off—she knew the genteel and proper way to do everything.

The tea and treats were, of course, not the purpose of the meeting. Following gracious protocol, Caroline and her mother were there by invitation, so they gracefully sipped their tea and took tiny bites from their biscuits and cakes, waiting for their hostess to make conversation.

It was a silent standoff as Caroline and her mother waited for the countess to make her assessment of them and begin the conversation.

Even though Caroline knew Bryne wouldn't join them, as teatime was exclusively for ladies, she couldn't help scanning the area unobtrusively to see if he was around.

Caroline's mother saw her and shot her a quick disapproving glance. Mothers didn't miss a thing. The countess also caught her glances and smirked, breaking the silence.

"You're quite taken with my Bryne, aren't you, Miss Stevens?"

"Yes, your grace," Caroline said sheepishly to conceal her error.

"He speaks well of your meeting at our ball," she said. "And Mrs. Stevens, I must tell you how much I admire your dress. And my sisters were merely agog by the stunning dress Miss Stevens wore to the ball. You must have a wonderful dressmaker."

"Thank you, Countess, but it's nothing in comparison to your grand home here," Mrs. Stevens said.

"That's so kind of you to say," the countess said.

The banality of conversation was stifling to Caroline, but she understood the process. Her mother spent hours drilling the protocol in great detail but experiencing the bouts of extreme silence was a little exasperating. She stayed the course and, although tempted, she resisted the urge to look around for Bryne even though every fiber of her being yearned to see him again.

"My son says your house is on the meadow in the south country," the Countess said.

"Yes, we have a few hundred acres and a fine house. We have come to enjoy the wonderful rolling hills," Mrs. Stevens replied.

"That's delightful. Sometimes the village area is a little confined," the Countess said.

"You must join us sometime to ride through the countryside," Mrs. Stevens said.

The endless tennis match of dull back-and-forth niceties was finally broken when Bryne came through the glass French doors.

"I'd like to ride through the hills with Miss Stevens anytime," he smiled and said, kissing his mother on the cheek. "Mother, may I whisk Miss Stevens away for a few minutes? I want to show her the grounds in the daylight."

The countess nodded and smiled at her son as he kissed her on the cheek. While it usually was a breach of etiquette to stroll through the gardens unaccompanied, Bryne knew his mother rarely denied anything to her favorite son.

Caroline thought he was her knight in shining armor, liberating her from the doldrums of afternoon tea. He looked the part in his riding costume with billowing white shirt, brown vest and high boots.

He took Caroline's hand and led her out the glass doors on his arm.

"I thought you'd need a rescue. Those teas are so tedious. I don't know how you lasted this long," he laughed.

"Thank you," Caroline giggled with ladylike restraint.

She wanted to tell him how glad she was to see him, how much she loved him and how his beautiful smiling face shined in the sunlight. But her mother taught her a lady said very little—that she must be quiet and act with proper refinement and control, so she just grinned at him adoringly.

"I thought a walk through the grounds would please you," he said.

Caroline looked up at him with doe-like eyes and smiled as she nodded. Any time spent in his company was fine with her, she thought.

As they strolled, she put both hands on his muscular arm and joyfully blushed at his side. She was never more content and knew she would be so happy with him always.

That night, Caroline met Maggie at their tree. She conveyed every detail of the tea and the walk afterward. Maggie listened ardently as Caroline recounted the events with intricate precision, illustrating everything and everyone meticulously. It was as if she were painting brushstrokes with words so Maggie could see it before her very eyes.

"Sounds a grand success. I'm so happy fer ya," Maggie said.

"I'm sure he'll propose any time now. Let's wish on a star for it." Caroline beamed and lay back on the grass, searching the deep blue sky for the brilliant moving celestial.

Their nightly tradition of wishing on a star evolved as they grew into young women, adding their hopes and dreams of a fantastic future.

"Wish, wish, shining star, make us be who we are. May ye glow on us every day, sprinkling dream dust to light our way. Whether far or near, show our heart's desire, 'til the day we say goodbye. And if ye take us far from ours, keep us forever Anam Cara."

Maggie lay back on the grass beside her. She was happy for her friend. Caroline was in love and would become mistress of a vast estate. And Maggie would be at her side, just like always. She took comfort in their lasting relationship. Even though they were grown now, nothing needed to change. They would remain friends forever.

─────── ༺༻ ───────

For the next few weeks, Caroline pranced around the house in a flurry of delight. Bryne called on her nearly every day to walk the grounds, ride horseback or take buggy rides into the village for dances or teas with his mother.

And Mrs. Stevens gladly gave her permission for each outing, gliding around the house with her chest puffed out, proud as a peacock that her daughter was being courted by Bryne Donegal, the seventh viscount.

Maggie didn't see Caroline much, but she was busy on her own secret project—the wedding dress.

She asked her mother if she could start on the wedding dress and a surprise trousseau for Caroline. The intricate hand-lacing on the veil alone would take weeks, especially with the length Caroline described.

Katherine spoke to Mrs. Stevens and she approved the order for the ivory satin and other materials needed. Given Countess Donegal's appreciation for the clothes Katherine and Maggie made, Mrs. Stevens insisted the wedding dress be the shining crown of their sewing achievements.

"I am trusting both of you," Mrs. Stevens said. "This dress must be the finest gown ever worn by a bride in the world. I want every woman there to be consumed with envy."

It was a tall order, but Maggie was equal to the task. Her skills were at the top of her game, and with no expense spared for the best materials, she would craft all her love into making Caroline the most beautiful bride to ever walk a church aisle.

They were all sure Bryne would propose any day.

Even though Caroline was busy, Maggie went to their tree spot every night to lie in the green and amber grass, look up at the starry night sky and think about Caroline, the dress and imagine the amazing adventures her friend was having. When Caroline had time, she would join her and tell stories about the people she and Bryne saw and the places they went.

Maggie heard about how Bryne was such a powerful rider, sitting straight and tall on the horse commanding it to prance and trot at his will. Caroline generously boasted of his graceful dancing, firmly placing his hand on her back, leading her around the dance floor, directing their waltz to the focus of everyone in the room.

Maggie was satisfied to hang on her every captivating word and dream of love and an amorous life through Caroline's enraptured eyes. As she listened to Caroline's sweeping tales of romance, she wondered if she was too hasty about men. She thought maybe it would be nice to experience that same feeling of all-encompassing infatuation for herself.

One night, as she was lying at the tree peacefully staring up at the sky, Maggie heard the echo of voices coming near—a man's baritone timbre and the faint giggle of a girl. As the sound drew nearer, she swiftly ran a few yards away and hid behind a nearby tree.

Two shadowy silhouettes came toward her. In the moonbeam, she glimpsed their faces. It was Caroline and Bryne.

At first, she was shocked and saddened to see Caroline bring him to their secret hideaway. But as she glanced at her grin in the moonlight, she knew it had to be special if that they were there alone in the night.

Maggie felt ashamed of her voyeurism, but as the surrounding fields were dark and open, she wasn't sure she could find her way back, unless she took their well-trodden path that led right past the secret tree spot. She had to stay but would remain hidden, so no one would know of her presence.

Caroline and Bryne lay beneath the tree as she showed him all the stars and constellations by name and what they meant. Over the years, Maggie and Caroline crafted tales of a menagerie of animals and people to describe the celestial bodies they watched nightly, like a play.

She wove the yarns with the expertise of a seanchaían, an old Irish storyteller, as Bryne lay quietly talking in every word.

Suzanne Rudd Hamilton

When Caroline explained their star wishing ritual to Bryne, Maggie was upset that she'd share their private tradition with him, as it made a personal bond between only them.

"You silly girl, your imagination is unlike any in the land," he chuckled. Then he leaned over, stroked her golden hair and kissed her full on the mouth.

Dazed from the kiss, Caroline uttered a pleasured sigh. Then he cradled her in his arms and kissed her again, longer this time, until there was no sound and Maggie thought neither could keep their breath.

He then swept Caroline off the grass and sat her against one of the trees, pressing her into the bark with the weight of his body against hers and kissing her forcefully with his hands on either side of her face. Caroline surrendered to him in complete submission as he untied her blouse and fondled her bosom, roughly caressing her and vigorously kissing her neck.

Stunned, Maggie looked away. Her green eyes could see no more. She was embarrassed that she witnessed such an intimate moment but was angry he was taking advantage of her outside the marriage bed.

Her ire built up to a boil as she closed her eyes and counted to three, as her mother always suggested. She took a deep breath and sighed, but after she opened her eyes, her anger remained ablaze. As she could take no more, Maggie sneaked away and stole into the night to get home one way or another.

൞

A few days later, Caroline met Maggie at the tree and described the encounter. Again, Caroline entwined beautiful ribbons in verse depicting his gentle touch against her cheek, his fingertips stroking her hair and his soft brief kiss on her lips.

Maggie said nothing and listened with one deaf ear as she remembered the steamier and less genteel version she witnessed. Even though Maggie was not knowledgeable of the proper practices of courtship and the allowances of intimate gestures between a young unmarried lad and lass, she was concerned Bryne was taking advantage of Caroline's naïve love and maiden youth in a way that could harm her.

No longer was Maggie transported into Caroline's adoring fantasy world of young love. As she let Caroline go on and on, she began to think her friend was lost in the delusion, with the promise of a forever love and no foot in the real world.

But she couldn't say anything. Caroline was in love and her mother wanted the influential marriage. It was not her place to tell the mistress of the house, even her best friend, how to live her life.

Maggie didn't go to the tree after that. She was afraid of encountering Caroline and Bryne there and after what she witnessed, she didn't want to know. She only hoped Caroline would not let his advances go too far.

She tried to evade any nearness to Bryne when he visited Caroline at Windemere, as the mere sound of his voice made her wince. She knew if she looked upon him, her green eyes would betray her true revulsion for him.

But she needed to squelch her personal feelings. Whether she agreed or not, there could be a wedding, as there was work to do. With some minor assistance from her mother, Maggie dutifully continued to create the beautiful wedding dress and trousseau each day. She loved Caroline and wanted her to take everyone's breath away, but her heart hardened to the marriage and left the task joyless.

A few weeks later, she heard loud jubilation in the house. Caroline and her mother were screaming with glee.

Maggie, Katherine, Mrs. O'Brien the cook and the butler Aaron all immediately ran into the dining room to see what the bother was. They found the two women dancing around.

"Maggie, I'm going to be a bride!" Caroline cried, elated and hugged her friend tightly. "I'm going to be a bride!"

She modeled the traditional Claddagh engagement ring—two hands holding a crowned heart. It was made of aged gold, but the traditionally unadorned ring was augmented with a large emerald in the heart and glimmering emeralds and diamonds in the crown and around the band.

"It's a family heirloom," she beamed with joy. "Isn't it glorious?"

Caroline grabbed her hands and danced around with Maggie.

Maggie could see the true glee in Caroline's sparkling blue eyes. She was consumed with Bryne's love and attention, so his proposal of marriage was her final threshold to a life of pure euphoria.

As Maggie looked into her friend's eyes, she spurned herself for doubting Bryne's intentions.

If his affection made Caroline this happy, she thought, how could it be wrong?

Maggie decided to turn over a new leaf in her notions of marriage and men. Despite what her eyes saw, her mind and heart must see him differently for Caroline's sake. It would be a grand affair and she was delighted to play a part.

Suzanne Rudd Hamilton

Chapter Four

For weeks after the joyous proposal, the house bustled with plans for the wedding. Caroline and her mother regularly went to tea with the countess to make all the necessary arrangements.

Lady Moira had a reputation throughout County Donegal for extravagant events. The wedding of Bryne's older brother, Robert, the count and his bride was legendary and created a high standard to uphold. So, this wedding would be a pinnacle event.

Maggie worked her fingertips bloody handcrafting the masterful gown and trousseau. She sewed tirelessly with needle and thread day and night, under a lone candle's glow, to complete the work.

Marrying into a wealthy family and living on a big estate, Caroline wouldn't need the household items of a normal trousseau; hers would be laden with belongings of a more personal nature. Of course, Caroline already had many fine custom dresses and gowns, made by Katherine and Maggie, which would be appropriate for her new position. And she had most of the general necessities of riding habit and outerwear, but her old personal lingerie was not suitable for a viscount's new bride, so Maggie focused on making delicate and pretty nightwear.

Mrs. Stevens purchased a new parasol, two hats and a ribbon-embroidered cloak from London and a beautiful hand-carved cedar chest topped with a light brocade fabric in Dublin to hold her personal items.

Mrs. Stevens asked Katherine to make a suit dress for Caroline, but Katherine spun and knit a shawl with intricate stitching and ribbons worthy of the finest dress houses for her own wedding present to Caroline.

For the trousseau, Maggie made two Swiss muslin nightgowns daintily trimmed with lace and satin ruffles at the collar and the sleeve cuff. Then she sewed a linen robe with a satin lapel and tie, made with remnants from the wedding gown.

And she embellished silk handkerchiefs with lace and hand-embroidered them with her friend's new initials—CSD as a wedding gift from her to her best friend. She saved material scraps from the fabrics Mrs. Stevens purchased but scrimped and saved for the special embroidery and lace threading.

Katherine and Maggie painstakingly hand-crocheted all the Irish lace themselves, detailing it with delicate flower motifs.

Caroline was a bundle of emotional extremes leading up to the wedding. She was happily busy at luncheons and teas, as the countess guided her through the elite women's circles of Ireland, but she was anxious to avoid any protocol lapses. And when she was home, she flittered about in a haze with bouts of pure happiness, fret about the wedding plans and nervousness about her new life.

She and Maggie hadn't been together for weeks, so the only time they talked was at fittings.

"I'm glad you'll be with me," Caroline said uneasily, biting her lip. "These people are very different. I'm constantly afraid of making a mistake or saying the wrong thing. I mostly just smile in silence for fear of an error."

Maggie stops putting pins in the dress for a bit and squeezes her friend's hand to comfort her.

"And their speech is so posh. Mother always reminds me to watch my country manners and phrases and speak as she taught me, but sometimes I slip. I probably sound like the maid to them," she said—and then immediately realized how it sounded and grabbed both Maggie's hand earnestly.

"Oh, sorry; you know I didn't mean anything. I'm just beside myself lately. Say you'll forgive me. Promise you'll be with me always."

Maggie smiled and nodded and began pinning the dress again. She felt no offense, as she knew Caroline was right. Their childhood closeness may have blurred the lines between their stations before, but they both knew under the critical gaze of her new circle, Caroline needed to elevate herself. She would no longer be the only child of a wealthy country landowner, but a viscountess of one of the richest aristocratic families in Ireland. And Maggie would no longer be her friend of her youth who worked in her home, but would be her personal lady's maid—her servant.

Before anyone knew it, the May 1st day of the wedding arrived.

Katherine told Maggie she was concerned the May date was a bad omen.

"They say marry when bees o'er May blossoms flit and strangers around your board will sit, and marry in the month of May, ya will surely rue the day."

Finally, the weeks of preparations had culminated in the finest event Mrs. Stevens and the countess could orchestrate.

On the morning of the wedding, Katherine told Maggie to check for the weather, listen hard for the sound of the cuckoo, and see if she could spot three magpies, another superstition to ensure the marriage would be a happy one.

Maggie dutifully looked, but paid little attention. While she always remembered and heeded much of her mothers' sayings, there were so many warnings in Irish folklore, Maggie thought a body could get twisted and turned just trying to prevent one thing and ensure another.

It was time to go to the church. Mrs. Stevens made special allowance for Katherine and Maggie to attend Caroline for the wedding and stay to witness the service at the back of the church; servants would normally not be permitted to attend. But with all the buttons and ties, it would take two of them to get Caroline into her dress.

As they entered the church, Maggie, Caroline and Katherine gasped in awe as they walked into the empty town's chapel, bursting with candelabras and candlesticks of white glowing candles and gorgeous floral arrangements of lilies, white roses, shamrocks and tall spikes of Bells of Ireland.

"This is the most gorgeous thing I've ever seen in me life. A garden aglow with dancing light on the inside," Maggie said, breathlessly sighing.

They slowly walked through the church sanctuary, gaping without a sound to reach the bride's chamber in the parish room, where they would dress Caroline. Maggie unveiled the finished wedding dress and displayed it to all for the first time. Although Katherine helped sew some pieces and Caroline saw bits from fittings, no one except Maggie laid eyes on the entire extravagant and expertly fashioned gown.

"Oh my!" Caroline shrieked, near tears when she saw the exquisite dress.

Maggie's months of tireless work were a success. Caroline would be the most beautiful bride ever to walk the aisle, stunning both the guild and gentry guests.

The gown was a masterpiece of skilled craftmanship, marrying the high station she was joining while highlighting Caroline's young innocence and subtle beauty.

The high collar was made with transparent delicate chiffon in ecru with vertical lines seamed to the scalloped top. The sheer chiffon dropped neck was separated from the lace-covered flounce. The vertical lines on the bodice gave a corseted look to the multi-ribboned waist. The wide skirt was made with shimmering ivory satin delicately covered by a sheer overskirt hand-embroidered with flowers.

The billowing chiffon sleeves puffed out as if air-filled, ending in the tight wrists lined with satin ribbon and trimmed with scalloped lace trim along the hands.

As Caroline requested, the veil had an eight-foot train so six maidens would carry it behind her. It was edged with satin ribbon and scallops of Irish lace. A coronet of traditional lavender flowers over the veil encircled her golden hair like a crown.

"You've outdone yourself. This is the grandest dress anyone has ever seen." Caroline hugged Maggie with tears in her eyes.

"Saints preserve us, fate is kind when a bride sheds tears on her wedding day," Katherine said, smiling, when Mrs. Stevens came in and saw them weeping.

"Enough with that now," Mrs. Stevens scolded. "Teary eyes make for puffy faces."

She stood marveling at her daughter in her wedding gown and smiled.

"You look perfect. But since you girls decided against the traditional blue, we needed something blue for you." She took a golden necklace with a petite sapphire from her purse and put it around Caroline's neck. It shined as brightly as her blue eyes.

"Good, we must keep traditions alive. Married in blue, he'll be true and married in white, 'tis alright," Katherine laughed. "Now we have something new and something blue. Ya have your mum's ear bobs for something borrowed and here's an old Irish penny for your shoe."

Maggie and Caroline looked at each other and laughed at the old traditions, but since it meant so much to their mothers, they obeyed.

Mr. Stevens came for Caroline as proud as a king in his blue dark frock coat and black top hat that matched the bridegroom. He smiled with his head held high and led her on his arm to walk to the vestibule, waiting for the processional to begin, after the vicar makes the ceremonial introductions. The bridesmaids, meanwhile, were busy gathering the veil's train.

Maggie and Katherine had to wait until everyone was in the chapel so they could stand in the back and witness the ceremony. Maggie looked down and realized she forgot her gloves in the parish room to cover her purple fingertips from the months of hand sewing.

As she passed the parish room, she saw Bryne and a dark-haired woman in a corner of the hall. Maggie quickly darted out of the way by a hair's breadth so she wouldn't be seen.

"I wish it were me," the dark-haired woman giggled as he pressed her against the wall.

"I wish it were you too," he said, grabbing and kissing her. "But you're not the woman I bring home to mother. We can have our fun while the dainty little country flower goes to teas and prances around as the viscountess."

Maggie's green eyes danced aflame with ire. Her face was so red, it matched her hair, but she couldn't say anything. She closed her eyes and counted to three and then breathed. She now knew her first feelings about Bryne were right.

"When ya see a snake, ya know his fangs are eventually going to bite," she mumbled under her breath.

She waited until they left, grabbed her gloves, and joined her mother. For everyone's sake, she had to keep the secret to herself.

Her simmering anger melted as she watched Caroline walk down the aisle and kneel with Bryne on the satin pillow at the altar.

Katherine was blubbering a little, and Maggie couldn't help but get teary-eyed herself as the ribbon was wrapped around Caroline and Bryne's wrists in a figure eight of infinity to hand fast their marriage in the Irish tradition of unity. A tear dripped down her cheek as she wept for her friend's happiness that may not come to pass and the prospect of their lives with this horrible man.

Walking home after the ceremony, she wouldn't tell her mother what she saw or why she was crying. She would tell no one.

With the knot tied, the bridal party and guests departed in a flurry of carriages to Donegal Hall for the wedding breakfast celebration.

The grand dining hall was laid with the finest crystal, silver and china atop the damask silk tablecloths.

A magnificent feast of mutton and salted corned beef with colcannon and boxty pancakes and individual meat pies was served with a mead honey-wine.

After the main meal, the footmen served the wedding fruitcake soaked in good Irish whiskey to the guests, while the butler placed the chocolate bridegroom cake in front of Caroline and Bryne for the cutting of the cake ritual. It was said the unmarried maid who received the longest piece would put the cake under her pillow and she would be the next to marry.

A bride's vanilla cake was packed away for the christening of their first child, per custom.

Caroline radiated throughout the wedding breakfast, but said nothing to keep her timid charade intact.

Mrs. Stevens was thoroughly enjoying her elevated station, bumping elbows with the richest of the Irish aristocracy, a position she hoped to cultivate and maintain as the mother of the viscountess.

However, Mr. Stevens was still a simple country gentleman who, to the dismay of Mrs. Stevens, vigorously indulged in the fine food during the wedding breakfast.

When the time for the speeches came and champagne was poured, Mr. Stevens rose to toast the health of the bride and groom.

"May there always be work for your hands to do; may your purse always hold a coin or two; may the sun always shine on your windowpane; may a rainbow be certain to follow each rain; may the hand of a friend always be near you; may God fill your heart with gladness to cheer you," he said and proudly raised his glass to the mildly bewildered quiet claps of the attendees.

When he sat, he found the icy stare of his wife searing through his face at his less than eloquent speech.

"Thank you, Mr. Stevens," said Bryne's brother Robert, the count, as he raised his glass to toast.

"May he bless your home with the peace that surpasses understanding. May your troubles be less and your blessings be more; and let nothing but happiness come in your door. Long live the Irish. Long live their cheer. Long live our family, year after year."

"Sláinte!" The rest of the guests rose and raised their glasses to toast the bride and bridegroom.

Suzanne Rudd Hamilton

Chapter Five

Caroline awoke the next morning alone in her Windemere bed, prepared to leave home for good.

Although most brides and bridegrooms lay together on their wedding night, the tired Caroline silently cried, overwhelmed with emotion when she saw her parents leaving after the wedding celebration. Seeing her sadness, Bryne graciously offered to allow her to spend her last night at her childhood home, which she happily accepted.

The next day was a solemn one; Caroline and Maggie were leaving home.

Mrs. Stevens seemed fine as she strutted around showing off the large Waterford crystal vase presented to Caroline by the dowager countess on the occasion of her wedding.

But as she walked around Windemere for the last time, Caroline was sad to leave her home, but knew it was the price of her new life and marriage to the man of her dreams.

Knowing her friend's prince was really the dirtiest of toads gave her no pleasure. She dreaded leaving her mother and feared life would be difficult for her, keeping this awful secret from Caroline.

As she packed her room, she sighed thinking of all the lies she would have to tell and crow she would have to eat to keep her Irish ire from bubbling up. She once hoped she was wrong about Bryne, but now had no doubt of the cad he was and why he married Caroline.

Maggie only hoped she could stand it, but she had to protect Caroline. She made a promise.

Katherine came into the room with tears in her eyes to see her daughter and the girl she loved like a daughter leave.

"It will be the worst of times for me with my wee bairn gone," Katherine said. "But ya both must fly on your own. And as a fancy lady's maid, you'll live in a fine house and live a fine life. Just remember, life will be different for ya. Caroline will be a mistress of the manor someday and even now, with her position, ya can no longer be the friends ya were. So, don't let your green Irish eyes betray you, no matter what, and remember to breathe."

"Now here." Katherine handed her a small box wrapped in a bow.

Filled with emotion, Maggie tore open the box. Inside was a lace collar and head cover with small black bows on each.

"A lady's maid in a grand house needs a proper uniform appropriate for her station," Katherine smiled. "I made the lace with your favorite flower, something to remember me by."

Maggie hugged her weeping mother and smiled. "I'm just going to the next county, Ma, not a different country. I'll be seeing ya."

Moving into Donegal Hall was a change for both Caroline and Maggie. They were interlopers, the new people who had to settle into established households, both upstairs and downstairs.

Caroline was moving into a family home with strangers. While she was familiar with them, she was in their territory. Her mother-in-law was the dowager countess, the matriarch. And her sister-in-law, Elizabeth, was the countess. Her husband was the second son and as the law provided, his brother Robert inherited the title, the estate, and the family's wealth. And as the wife of the viscount, she had a title, but no position in the household.

As Caroline's maid, Maggie's duties were clear. She dressed and attended to Caroline and her personal wardrobe and needs, nothing more. And as a lady's maid in a large household, she ranked only above maids and footmen on the third tier of the servant hierarchy. But she was new to the other servants and the surroundings and didn't know how she would be received.

The carriage pulled up to the front steps of the estate. Caroline and Maggie both paused, looking up at the grandeur of the home, each with a daunting feeling.

Suzanne Rudd Hamilton

Caroline's earlier trips seemed fleeting and less intimidating. This was real. It was their home now.

"Welcome to your new home, ma'am," Gallagher the butler said and instructed the footmen to get Caroline's bags.

"Donnelly, the servant's entrance is in the rear. Mrs. Doyle will show you to your room," he ordered.

Caroline shot Maggie a frightened look as they were ushered down from the carriage. She would have to enter the home alone.

She followed Gallagher into the sitting room, where her mother-in-law and sister-in-law were waiting.

"Dear, please sit down and be comfortable," Lady Moira said and poured her some tea. "We want you to feel at home here."

"Mrs. Doyle, our housekeeper, had your room made up and the footmen will have your luggage delivered to your room so your lady's maid will have everything sorted and you can change for dinner."

"Thank you, Maggie will know what to do," Caroline happily said.

"Maggie?" Elizabeth asked, shocked.

"Caroline, there will be many adjustments and things to learn in your new life. Not to worry, Elizabeth and I will guide you through. But we always call our ladies' maids by their last names."

"Oh, sorry," Caroline said, embarrassed, and lowered her head to take a sip of tea.

Downstairs, Maggie felt similarly naïve confronted with the ways of a big estate. Mrs. Doyle, the housekeeper, was waiting for her at the back door and quickly shuttled her up the stairs to her room in a whirlwind.

"Now hurry, Donnelly," Mrs. Doyle said, hurriedly ushering Maggie up the stairs. "The viscountess is at tea with the countesses. She will need everything in her room unpacked and settled so you can dress her for dinner. Your uniform is on the bed. I'll come back in five minutes to show you to your mistress's room."

Maggie looked around the room. It was small and plain with all white walls and a simple white quilted bedspread with a dresser, but at least it was hers alone. She saw the fancy dark black uniform dress on her bed and quickly changed. She would unpack later and add the lace trim her mother made, so she closed the door and scurried down the stairs to an awaiting Mrs. Doyle.

Mrs. Doyle was a spry middle-aged woman with sandy brown hair and a few single gray stands showing. She walked at a racehorse's pace through the servants' area to the upstairs of the estate home. Following her quick gait, Maggie was nearly out of breath when she opened the enormous wooden door to Caroline's room.

Maggie's jaw dropped and she gasped at the majesty of the room. It was a field of yellow from the brocade wallpaper to the luxurious damask drapes to the oriental rug. The raised canopy bed was fit for a queen, with fringe trim on the matching canopy and privacy curtains.

"It's like you've never seen a room before, my girl; close your jaw and listen," Mrs. Doyle said.

She hurriedly bustled about the room as if in a race, explaining where to properly place things. Maggie listened while she snuck glances at the room, still in awe of its opulence.

"I will take my leave. I heard you and the viscountess are friends, but that will change. This household adheres to the strictest decorum. You must keep a proper separation between you and your mistress. And you must always refer to her as viscountess," Mrs. Doyle snapped and closed the door behind her.

Maggie was stunned at the grandeur room and the coolness of the reception she received, but busied about unpacking Caroline's things and putting them away. Two hours later, Gallagher escorted Caroline into the room, standing straight as a board at the entry, showing all the pomp his position and her title dictated in a proper household.

"Your room, viscountess," Gallagher said and showed Caroline inside and promptly closed the door.

Caroline and Maggie looked at each other and burst into laughter at his strict adherence to a ceremony completely foreign to both of them.

Caroline's reaction to the room parroted Maggie's. She slowly spun around the room, gaping at the spectacular décor, and then smiled at Maggie and laughed again.

"I've never seen anything like this in my life," Caroline giggled and plopped on the bed.

"I know. It's nearly as blinding as the sun in here," Maggie snickered. "Would the viscountess like to change for dinner?"

"Don't be daft, Maggie. It's just us here," Caroline said.

"Not on your life. That Mrs. Doyle is bound to have her ear right at the keyhole. I have already been warned about the observances in this house and I don't want to find meself in the dungeon, thank you very much."

"This home doesn't have a dungeon, silly," Caroline laughed. "But I know what you mean. Protocol is so important to them. I have been informed I need to call you Donnelly from now on. I hope all these changes don't steal the life from us."

"Well, if ya don't mind me saying so, these are serious people and I think we need to follow where they lead. And if it's Mrs. Doyle, ya need to go quick. She walks like the devil himself is after her," Maggie said, and they both laughed again.

Everyday dinner at Donegal Hall was slightly less grand than Caroline's wedding breakfast and the parties she attended there with only four courses of soup, beef, vegetables and dessert. But with her earlier faux pax at tea, using the wrong name for Maggie, Caroline was even more guarded against making any mistakes, so she sat quietly throughout each dinner course, closely watching and imitating every move the dowager countess made.

Too busy concentrating, she barely listened to the conversation at the table until the footmen cleared the final plates and Lady Moira addressed her directly.

"How are you settling in, dear? I trust your accommodation is acceptable," she asked.

"Everything is wonderful, thank you. Dinner and the room," Caroline replied softly.

"Mother thought the bright yellow color would make you feel more at home, like in the country," Elizabeth sneered with slight sarcasm and disdain, disrespectfully looking away from Caroline when she spoke to her.

"I'm sure the ladies of the house will grant you any time needed to become accustomed to the routine," Robert said coolly. "Now, if you ladies will excuse us, Bryne and I will adjourn for cigars and brandy."

Caroline was puzzled by his pronouncement. Although it was typical for the men and women to adjourn separately after dinner, she hadn't been alone with Bryne all day and yearned for some private close time to be together as a newly married couple. Especially as he allowed her to break with tradition and sleep at Windemere on their wedding night, this was their first chance to be man and wife and she was now ready and very willing to begin her wifely duties.

Bryne saw the look of confusion and disappointment on her face. "Don't worry, little bird; I will come and see you this night," he said softly and kissed her on the forehead.

"Girls, we can enjoy some music and sherry in the drawing room," Lady Moira said.

Caroline followed and daydreamed about her first night with Bryne as his wife.

After everyone retired, Caroline regally walked up to her room, while inside she was prancing, thrilled to finally become a woman.

"Maggie, pick out the prettiest nightgown you made me, maybe the flowy one with the ribbons," Caroline said, bursting with excitement. "Do you think I should lace my hair in ribbons or keep it loose?"

"Just one ribbon in a bow at the top, I think. Your hair is so pretty when its unbound." Maggie faked a smile. She couldn't help but be washed away in Caroline's glee, but she still distrusted Bryne.

His gallant gesture, not forcing himself on her for their wedding night, surprised and pleased Maggie, making her think twice about the true depth of his character. But the vision at the church of him with the dark-haired woman right before he took his vows still haunted her mind. He was obviously no stranger to lovemaking and as she left Caroline alone in the room, Maggie hoped he would consider his bride's innocence and delicacy.

Caroline fidgeted on her enormous canopy bed in quiet anticipation among the candles that gave the dark room an amber hue of romantic glow. She imagined this night ever since Bryne first kissed her and the anticipation bubbled over in her mind.

A few minutes after Maggie left, Bryne thrust open the door.

"Little bird, are you ready for me?" he proclaimed with a wide grin.

"Yes, oh yes," Caroline exclaimed softly.

He smiled and walked toward her, standing next to the bed and removing his red velvet robe to reveal his muscular toned body. Caroline sighed, as she had only seen his muscular arms and legs under his shirt and riding tods. She beamed, seeing his rippling hairy chest for the first time.

He met her wanting gaze and looked upon her sitting virginally against the pillows.

"You won't be needing any of this," he smiled with a slight chuckle as he gently removed her nightgown, leaving only her alabaster skin blending with the white linens.

Caroline was breathless and enraptured as he gradually stroked his hands up and down, caressing and kissing every part of her body, leaving her trembling and tingling from every pore.

She was in a trance of ecstasy as he laid atop her with his body melding with her own, gasping as he held her tightly and slowly made love to her.

She closed her eyes in a dreamlike state, while he touched and kissed her, holding his sweaty body close against her skin. She cooed and huffed while he orchestrated one pleasant act after another, pressing his body into hers, so she barely knew where she ended and he began.

When it was over, she sighed and smiled, bathed in sheer contentment. She never felt so fully at one with another and was so deeply in love with his amorous attentions, she wondered if anything could feel so delightful.

"I'm glad you enjoyed it." Bryne sat up with a satisfied grin and put on his robe, leaving her lying hazy on the bed.

"Aren't you going to stay, my darling?" she asked, still partially in her blissful stupor.

"That's not the way it's done," he smiled, kissing her forehead. "I have my own room, little bird; I'll come to see you at night. Now I'll leave you to rest your pretty head."

The morning glow peeked through the yellow curtains until Maggie yanked them open, shining one beam of bright light on Caroline's bare body.

"Oh," Caroline exclaimed when she awoke and realized her nakedness, quickly covering herself with the sheet.

"I trust it was a successful night," Maggie said, nodding, and handed her the robe.

Caroline put on her robe and sat up in the bed smiling. "It was simply wonderful," she sighed.

"I have your breakfast tray right here," Maggie said.

"Don't I get dressed for breakfast?" she asked.

Maggie shook her head and shrugged, placing the tray in front of her.

"I was surprised too, but Mrs. Doyle says the married ladies of the house have a tray brought to them to eat in bed."

Caroline smiled in acceptance and ravenously tore through her breakfast. When she finished, she glanced out the window and saw Bryne walking to the stables. She jumped out of bed and instantly changed into her riding pants, boots and jacket and ran outside to join him.

Elizabeth and Lady Moira were working on their needlepoint in the sitting room when Elizabeth looked out the window and noticed Caroline running fast out the front door toward Bryne as he led his horse out of the stables.

"Mother, Caroline is in riding breeches?" she gasped in shock.

The dowager countess looked out the window and chuckled at Caroline's exuberant innocence.

"Well, there's a lot to learn, but give her time."

Elizabeth didn't accept her sister-in-law's etiquette oversights as easily. She thought Bryne married beneath his station; although Caroline's family was wealthy, they were country people.

Her own lineage was from the Irish aristocracy. Neither she nor Robert was comfortable with Caroline and Bryne living in the house and each made them aware of it at every opportunity.

Downstairs, Maggie brought Caroline's empty tray down to the kitchen and sat down at the kitchen table for her own breakfast when she overheard the scullery maids quietly talking.

"There's not a morsel left on the new mistress's plate today," one maid snickered.

"Guess it's true what they say about Mr. Bryne and his nighttime activities," the other maid giggled.

"I would be hungry too, if I was busy like that two nights in a row," the first one said and they both snickered.

Puzzled, Maggie thought about what they said while waiting for the others to join and begin breakfast. Since this was their first night together, what did they mean by two nights busy?

Did Bryne sleep with someone else here on his wedding night?

She shook her head with disgust just thinking about it. Every time she gave Bryne another chance, he proved himself unworthy. Although she had little information, she had no problem believing he was unfaithful.

As Mr. Gallagher and Mrs. Doyle entered the room, everyone at the table rose and then sat to begin eating, just as they did for every meal.

The large Donegal household of servants was so regimented, Maggie felt like she enlisted in her majesty's army. Gallagher and Mrs. Doyle ran an exacting schedule with specific protocols and procedures for everything.

Learning all their rules was exhausting. But on Sundays, Maggie was given half day off, so she and Katherine could go to church together and have lunch at Windermere. She vented her frustrations about the Donegal domestics and Bryne, while no one was around to overhear.

"It's a curse of Irish women to love their men fiercely and for Irish men to be cursed to plant their seed in many flowers. We all share that burden, but only some of us make peace with it," Katherine said.

"But as for the others, me girl, in the land of the blind, the one-eyed man is king. Ya have a unique set of skills. Show them who you are and they'll follow ya anywhere," Katherine told her.

Maggie was a quick study and good judge of people. While she didn't agree with her mother about men, she understood her why her scorned past, raising a daughter without a father, led her to that belief. But she was determined to step in line and fit in for Caroline's sake.

Heeding Katherine's advice, she found little charming ways to ingratiate herself with Mrs. Doyle and the other servants.

She made them little bows for their uniforms or mop caps. She made Mrs. Doyle a lace collar for her uniform, like the one her mother had made for her, but bigger considering her position. For Gallagher's birthday, she embroidered his initials on his handkerchiefs. And she turned no one down to sew a button or mend a jacket.

Soon Maggie endeared herself in the downstairs commune. But after several months in the house, Caroline believed she would never please her in-laws.

"I think Elizabeth hates me," she told Maggie. "She always puckers her face at me and never offers any notions of friendship. I've tried so hard to do things their way, but they are so stiff. I'm just glad I have you with me. You're my only friend."

"I'm afraid she'll always think of ya as the sow's ear and not the silk purse," Maggie warned. "She's from their ways and as much as ya try, she may not accept you."

"And I hardly see Bryne. He's away at Derry City so much for work, he only has time for me on weekends. We've only been riding and to the beach a few times. He's attentive to his husbandly duties—every night he's here—but I'm so lonely without him," she said, with tears streaming down her face.

Maggie comforted her but worried that given Bryne's past misdoings, her friend would stay lonely in this enormous palace. She heard chatter from the babbling scullery maids that Elizabeth and Robert didn't want Caroline and Bryne in the house, but the Lady Moira favored Bryne and liked Caroline's sweet spirit.

A few weeks later, Maggie found Caroline sitting alone in the middle of the room in the morning with her head in the washbasin. She looked paler than usual and could barely lift her arms.

Concerned, Maggie put her into bed and put a cold cloth on her head. Then she went down to ask Mrs. Doyle for help.

"I'm very worried about the viscountess," Maggie urged. "I've never seen her this sick in her whole life. She's been tired for the last few weeks and eats very little. Can someone fetch the doctor?"

Maggie was confused when Mrs. Doyle and the cook, Mrs. Sullivan, smiled at her.

"No need for a doctor, my girl," Mrs. Sullivan laughed heartily. "The only thing you need to worry about is preparing for the wee babe. I'll make her some soda bread and tea."

"A baby?" Maggie was bewildered but excited. She had very little knowledge or experience with anyone in the family way. She raced up the stairs and ran up to Caroline to tell her the news.

"Caroline!" she screamed, catching her breath. "You're up the pole. We're having a wee bairn!"

Caroline could barely hold up her head from the pillow. "What?" she asked, confused at first. "A babe?" She smiled and lay her head back.

When Bryne came home on the Friday, Caroline told him of the baby. He was thrilled to have an heir and joyously announced it to the whole family.

Robert and Elizabeth, who had yet to conceive after two years of marriage, were less than congratulatory, but the dowager countess was elated and began making plans for a new Donegal in the nursery.

One of the maids told Maggie she overheard Elizabeth tell Robert she wasn't surprised that the country girl would be expecting so soon.

"The young countess said 'it's that country breeding. They're fertile like farm animals.'

Considering the real threat to Elizabeth and Robert's family position if they were unable to produce an heir, Caroline ignored their sarcastic quips and jabs and basked in the glowing glee at being a mother.

As soon as her sickness passed, she had Mrs. Stevens for tea with Lady Moira to tell her about the expectant birth.

And when Maggie told her mother at Sunday lunch, Katherine cried and immediately got to work on crocheting booties and caps and sewing a fine layette for the babe.

༺༻

Over the next months, Mrs. Stevens attended many teas at Donegal Hall with Caroline and Lady Moira, making plans for the nursery and christening celebration. A Donegal heir would not come into the world with a whimper, but with a joyous celebration.

Lady Moira was so excited about the new heir, she constantly doted on Caroline as if she were her own daughter, leaving Elizabeth completely alone and resentful. They shopped in town together and sat around at night chatting and laughing. Lady Moira loved Caroline's youthful innocence and exuberance.

Caroline was so busy with bustling around with arrangements for the baby's arrival, she barely noticed Bryne's nightly absences. He told her he was working on a big business deal for their future, so he would be staying in the city a lot. As the second son, he didn't inherit the family's wealth.

Maggie couldn't help but think his abandonment had less to do with work and more to do with his heightened extracurricular activities, as his wife was indisposed and unable to meet his nightly carnal needs.

But they hardly missed him. Maggie and Caroline were like schoolgirls fluttering around on clouds once again, preparing to tend to their baby. And apart from the permanent scowl on Elizabeth's face, for months Donegal Hall was overflowing with anticipation and happiness.

Seven months later, a baby girl came, and they named her Moira, after the dowager countess. Caroline, Bryne and both families proudly held the christening celebration and elaborate luncheon. The bride's cake from their wedding was cut into small bits and served to the guests.

The nursery was filled with gifts and warmth. Katherine came over after the celebration to see the babe and Maggie snuck her into the nursery. She wept with joy at the next generation come to life.

"Someday, you'll have one of your own with red hair and green eyes like a true Donnelly," Katherine boasted holding the babe.

"Maybe. Someday. I'll have a lot to do before then. Too bad ya need a man to get one," Maggie said. "For now, I'll love Moira like me own girl."

Bryne doted on little Moira. He never missed an opportunity to play with her in the nursery and brought her gifts every time he was home. Caroline was depressed at the attention he lavished on the baby girl and jealously neglected her.

When Bryne brought a little toy bird that moved back and forth and called Moira his "little bird," Caroline cried for days in a dark room. She wouldn't see Moira and didn't eat more than a scrap of bread.

"I'm just a mare to him and he's the prize stud," she cried on Maggie's lap. "He still comes in every night. He's here to be with me, but it's faster and faster every time. He says he wants more children right away, but there's no intimacy. He just does his business and then off to his room with himself."

Maggie stroked Caroline's hair, consoling her, even though she expected as much. She knew Bryne never loved her friend, but she hoped Caroline's adoration would be enough.

"Me mother says, a little fire that warms is better than a big fire that burns. And it's a well-known principle that if ya keep the flint in one drawer and the steel in the other, you'll never strike much of a fire," Maggie said, reassuring her. "His head is full of being a new father. It will pass and he'll come back to you."

Maggie didn't believe a word she said, but couldn't see Caroline in that state. She wanted to give her hope that all would be better.

Caroline slowly came out of her misery and began to perk up. When Moira was two months old, Bryne came back one Friday night and gathered the whole family before dinner for a big announcement.

"I've been offered a new job in New York to work for a railroad company," he declared. "We're moving to America."

Suzanne Rudd Hamilton

Chapter Six

Caroline was stunned.

Just like that, they were moving a world away. No discussion. She, Moira, Bryne and Maggie would have an ocean between everything and anything they had ever known and loved.

Robert and Elizabeth jumped up and clapped, congratulating Bryne. They were ecstatic to have the viscount, viscountess and their heir out of their hair.

Lady Moira was silent. She sat straight up in her chair with sad eyes, holding back tears. Her favorite son, new daughter and her only grandchild would be gone, but she realized there was nothing she could do.

"Isn't that great, Caroline? New York has a bustling society scene. I'm envious," Elizabeth said with a façade. She was happy. Happy that Caroline would be out and she would be without competition for the dowager's favors.

Ever since Moira was born, Elizabeth was stuck in the back seat looking on, with the baby and her mother getting all the attention.

Caroline sat like a statue in shock. She didn't react or say anything.

"She's going to love America," Bryne stood behind her chair with his hand on her shoulder in solidarity, without looking in her direction or caring about her reaction.

After dinner, Lady Moira stoically excused herself to grieve in private. As there were no ladies sherry and cards that night, it gave Caroline a chance to breathe in her room and tell Maggie.

"He didn't even ask," Caroline cried on Maggie's lap. "He just proclaimed that we're moving across the world and I can say nothing. I have no part in any decision of my life because he's the man and I'm his wife."

Maggie comforted Caroline, but she was terrified. Caroline didn't have a choice, but she did. While she consoled Caroline, her mind wandered. Did she want to go to America? Leave her mother and her country? But what about Caroline and Moira? They were her family too. She promised Caroline she would never leave her.

Suddenly, Caroline looked up at her with her wet face and eyes in terror. "You're coming with us, right? You have to. I can't do this alone. A new country. New places. New people. Please, I need you," she begged Maggie.

Maggie looked down at her pitiful expression and her heart melted. "Of course, I'll go with you. Remember, Anam Cara."

As soon as Maggie uttered the words "I'll go," she felt a lump in her throat. She would probably never see her mother or the Emerald Isle again. But how could she say no?

"As me mother says, two people shorten the road. I'll always be with you. We've tackled change before and we'll do it again. It will be an adventure for us all." Maggie dried Caroline's face with a handkerchief. "Bryne will be here soon to say goodnight. We need to get ya ready."

Caroline calmed down, knowing Maggie would be with her, but soured about Bryne.

"I have to get ready for him, so he can busy himself on top of me for fifteen minutes and leave. Children may be a blessing from our Lord but making them can be a curse."

"You're upset and making a pot of gold sound like a rock," Maggie said to comfort her. "Changing times makes everyone look a lot of ways. Once you're all happy in America, it will be better."

Maggie swiftly left Caroline's room so she wouldn't choke on her words. When she closed the door, she made the sign of the cross on her head and chest and whispered to herself.

"God forgive me and help me. Where the tongue slips, it speaks the truth. Make my devil lies sing like angels. It's better she believes. Honesty won't change anything."

Downstairs, the news traveled like lightning. By breakfast, the household staff knew of the move. Maggie just sat there eating with a smile on her face, nodding at all the chitter chatter about America.

"I hear there are so many people in New York, ya can't even move," one of the footman said.

"You're daft; America is the most wonderful place in the world," a young maid scolded the footman and then earnestly told Maggie. "You can be anything there."

"Yes, anyone is free in America to be a servant," another footman said.

"I hear the buildings reach to the heavens," Mrs. Sullivan said.

"I'm sure the viscount will acquire the finest home," Gallagher said. "It will be a marvelous opportunity for you, my dear."

She took everything they said and added it to the whirlwind in her own mind. A new house. New people. New country. It was both exciting and daunting, but regardless, she knew for Caroline and Moira, she needed to remain steadfast and cheerful about the move.

After breakfast, she got up to tend to her sewing, but Mrs. Doyle gently grabbed her arm and pulled her into the other room.

"I can't understand what you must be going through, my girl. But the mark of a good maid is her service and loyalty to her missus. You do us all proud."

Maggie thanked her for her praise and went up to her room. She felt better knowing someone understood her sacrifice.

෨ඏ

A month later, all packed and ready to leave for America, Maggie, Caroline and Moira went to Windermere to say goodbye to their family before they departed.

Mrs. Stevens was bouncing around with Moira as if it were a happy occasion.

"You all will be so happy in America. The society people there love the aristocracy. Your title is your calling card to Millionaire's Row. You will exist in the lap of luxury," she perked with excitement.

Caroline was not as sure as her mother or as happy to bid them goodbye, but she knew on her wedding day that Windermere was a part of her past. She ardently looked around each room as if she were burning the images into her memory.

"You and Father can come visit us in America," she said hopefully.

"Yes, of course," Mrs. Stevens said nonchalantly to pacify her daughter, but they both knew a trip across the pond for a visit was not likely.

Maggie and Katherine were alone in the kitchen, having a cup of tea. They were both solemn and tearful. They knew they would never see each other again.

"I have something for you." Katherine wiped her tears and handed Maggie a box with a bow.

Maggie smiled at her and pulled at the ribbon to open the box. Inside was a straw hat with a green and white striped ribbon and bow on the back.

"Ya need a proper hat for your travels across the sea," Katherine said tearily.

Maggie hugged her. "Don't cry, Ma. As ya always say, Irish families are connected heart to heart. Neither time nor distance can keep them apart."

"Me darling daughter, may the most ya wish for be the least ya get," Katherine kissed her forehead.

"I will write to you, soes ya won't even miss me," Maggie said, waving goodbye as she, Caroline, and Moira walked out the door of Windermere for the last time.

The departure from Donegal Hall was slightly different. Elizabeth, Robert and Lady Moira stood in the grand foyer as they were about to leave.

Elizabeth and Robert wore Cheshire grins as they kept up a pretense of regret at the parting. Maggie thought they would probably dance a jig before their dust even settled.

The dowager countess was sad, but she prepared herself for this. As a lady of her station, her back was straight and poised with no visual outpouring of emotion.

"America will be a wonderful new challenge for all of you. Go with my good wishes and blessings." She kissed

Moira's forehead, nodded at Caroline and stood there with her dignified mask, hiding her sorrow.

The entire staff was standing at attention by the carriage to bid them goodbye. They nodded silently as Caroline, Bryne, and Moira walked out the door past them into the carriage. Maggie saw Gallagher and Mrs. Doyle look at her with kind eyes. She appreciated their admiration and hoped the next household would afford her equal respect.

They journeyed by train to the shipyard in Derry for the ten-day voyage. Maggie knew this journey was going to be difficult emotionally and physically, especially for Caroline. Right before the crossing, Caroline found out she was with child again and between her condition and the rough sailing, she was pale and weak for the entire journey.

Day and night, Maggie tended to her and Moira. They never left their suite and Caroline barely moved from her bed, so Maggie played with Moira and kept her occupied while spoon-feeding Carolina broth and crackers to keep her alive. Meanwhile, Bryne enjoyed everything the ship had to offer, including games on the deck, fine dining with the rich passengers and cards, cigars and brandy with the men in the ship's smoking rooms. He rarely returned before the wee hours of the morning.

But Maggie suspected he was cajoling and chasing women around. When she was picking up his discarded coat to have it laundered on the ship, she found a lace handkerchief marked by lipstick and scented with perfume in his coat pocket.

"It's like the elephant sitting in the front room and no one sees it," she said to herself with disgust and disposed of the handkerchief before Caroline could see it.

As they approached New York Harbor, Maggie gawked in awe of the majestic and newly erected Statue of Liberty. She took in the marvelous view Mrs. Sullivan, talked about with buildings that reached to the heavens. With the fluffy white clouds hovering atop the buildings, Maggie thought the city looked like the stairway to the pearly gates.

When they disembarked, the harbor was chaotic with pursers and uniformed men yelling orders in every direction at the huddled and confused second and third-class passengers, while the first-class passengers were gently escorted to waiting carriages. Bryne's company made arrangements for him, Caroline and Moira to be preprocessed through immigration and have their trunks sent ahead to the house in New York. Maggie, however, was hastily directed to the immigration center for processing.

At first Caroline objected to their separation from Maggie, but Bryne looked at her sternly and explained, "This is just the way they do things here. Maggie will be fine."

He handed Maggie an envelope. "Here are your employment papers, our address and fare for the trolley. You can come to the house when you are done."

Suzanne Rudd Hamilton

Caroline and Moira waved goodbye to Maggie as their carriage quickly disappeared into the packed crowds. Left by herself, Maggie was immediately shuttled to an endless line of people, carrying her suitcase and purse, in step with the hopeful hordes of others from all parts of the globe.

She stood there frightened and unsure, mindlessly following the person in front of her, awaiting direction. Looking around, she saw people in all manner of native costumes revealing their homelands, each carrying one or two pieces of luggage for a whole family. She stared down at her bag and felt privileged that she had more than so many.

One man wore a green hat with a large feather in it. A family with several women wore shawls around their heads that tied at their chins. She heard a lady call it a babushka.

People were quietly chattering to one another in different languages. It was both interesting and terrifying. She had a certain curiosity about people and worlds she never knew existed, but at the same time felt like a small pea swallowed in a large mattress.

Everyone seemed as oblivious as she was, merely doing what they were told, shifting in time with the crowd as if it were one orchestrated movement.

When she got to the front, a very surly man rapidly shouted questions at her in succession, scaring her to breathlessness.

"Papers! Destination! Name! Sponsor!"

Maggie sheepishly handed him the envelope Bryne gave her and looked at him with terrified saucer eyes.

"Name!" he screamed at her.

"Maggie, uh, Mary Margaret Katherine Anne Donnelly," she blurted.

"In America you can only have three names. Pick three now!" he yelled.

"Margaret Katherine Donnelly," she mumbled.

He violently stamped the papers and shoved them loosely at her, while tersely bellowing for the next in line. She was confused and didn't know where to go, but a strange man pushed her out of the way to get to the attendant, nearing knocking her down.

Maggie was in a daze. Only a few hours in America and she had a new name and would immediately need to navigate the unknown to her new home.

Determined, she knew she had only herself to rely on. She shook her head and forced her way through the crowd, then asked a uniformed man to direct her to the trolley. She showed the driver where she was going—1 W 72nd Street, The Dakota, Central Park West.

Maggie stood holding onto the horse-drawn trolley, bouncing her head back and forth, trying to take everything in her view. It was miraculous.

Suzanne Rudd Hamilton

The streets were lined with rows of townhomes and buildings stuck together as far as the eye could see. Carriages and people filled the streets up and down the walks.

Even the largest city in County Donegal paled in comparison to this urban wonderland with more people in her eyeshot than all in the county.

She was astonished at every vista in scope marking off the gloriously ornate buildings as they sped by.

The trolley left off a few blocks from the address and she followed 72nd Street until she reached the corner.

She walked along in amazement, wondering how all these people could fit in one city and where they were all going. But as she got closer, the crowds thinned and the streets were open, except for a carriage here and there. The buildings aside the street diminished as well.

On the other side of the street, she saw an empty grassy area with a few trees, an open plain amidst a roaring metropolis. The vast field seemed sorely out of place, but Maggie cheerfully paused and stared at it with comfort and ease. That was the only grass she'd seen since she left Ireland.

Finally, she came to the corner and peered her first glimpse at the Dakota. She stopped and gasped at the towering magnificence of the enormous building that would be her new home.

The brand-new hulking structure measured eight stories tall and one block long and was treated with every adornment and embellishment that appealed to discerning and wealthy occupants.

Maggie raised her eyes up and down in awe. She couldn't help standing in silence gaping at every nook and cranny noticing every detail of the ledges, balconies, columns, archways and decorative iron railings, planters and urns. The slate and copper roof punctuated with gables and turrets, and finial-topped peaks reminded her of the old county building in Derry and some others she observed on the Trolley ride. But none of them had everything. She smiled and puffed out her chest a bit, proud that she was to live in the most beautiful building in New York.

She thought it was like the perfect dress, taking excellence from many designs and weaving it into the most beautiful frock in the world.

Walking toward the arched porte cochère entrance, Maggie and slowly looked around, confused about where to go, when a curt man yelled at her for loitering.

"The servant's entrance is on 73rd Street!" he barked.

She walked the block around the corner with her eyes opened wide, gaping at each stunning aspect of the endless building until she came upon the domestic entry door.

This was it. She took a deep breath and opened the door to a new home and the new world that awaited.

Suzanne Rudd Hamilton

Chapter Seven

Fall 1889

Once inside, she immediately found the stairway to carry her to the fourth-floor apartment in the Dakota.

Maggie entered the kitchen and butler's pantry from the back hallway. She wandered around in astonished at the shiny newness of everything in the home, just like she hoped America would be.

"You must be Mrs. Donnelly," the butler said. "You may call me Mr. Gordan."

He was in his early forties, with brown hair and sullen grayish skin. A proper butler, he was stoic in his demeanor and postured his tall figure like a steel pole without bend.

"Pleased to meet you, Mr. Gordan, but ya must be mistaken. I'm Maggie Donnelly. Mrs. Donnelly's me mother," she smiled while correcting him.

Mr. Gordan sighed deeply and looked at her with a hint of noticeable intolerance.

"My dear Mrs. Donnelly, I am aware you are unwed, but in a proper household, the housekeepers are always known as Mrs.," he said.

"Housekeeper?" Maggie asked in stunned confusion.

Mr. Gordan instantly saw that Maggie was not informed of the household compliment and lighten his tone.

"Mrs. Carmichael, the Irish cook, and I were engaged by Viscount Donegal's employer. We were told the viscountess traveled with her head of household, who would engage further domestic help," he explained.

Maggie was speechless and could feel a little panic and ire bubble up. She was mad Bryne assumed he could put her in any position he needed and scared she was in a situation where she would have responsibility over others. She didn't know if she was ready for that. And she didn't know if she wanted to be.

She wondered if Caroline knew about her new position, but immediately dismissed that notion. She suspected Bryne concocted it on his own and said nothing to his wife so there would be no objection.

"Well, as me mother always says, no use thinking when there's work to be done, so best get on with it," she said, taking a deep cleansing breath.

"Very well; let me show you to your room. Most of the servants are housed in the building's servants' quarters on the 8th and 9th floors, but there is one domestic room here in the residence. The viscount insisted this room be yours," he said, and showed her to her room.

"Thank you, Mr. Gordan," she said as he left and scanned the room.

It was similar in size to her room at Donegal Hall and Windermere, but just like the kitchen, everything was modern. The windowless room had a big wooden secretary desk, small wardrobe cabinet with drawers and in the corner lay a brand-new sewing machine with table and padded chair.

Maggie drew right to it like a magnet. She'd heard about automatic sewing machines in downstairs gossip, but never dreamed of having one. She touched every part of it, grinning in pure astonishment, and envisioned all the wonderful garments she could craft with such a brilliant device.

"Bryne wanted to surprise you," Caroline said, interrupting her. "It's a gift for coming here for us."

A jolt of shock resonated through her body, perplexing her yet again. Bryne made her this amazing present? Bryne Donegal?

Caroline giggled and grabbed Maggie's hand.

"I know this is all a lot to take in. I didn't know you'd be the housekeeper, but the staff is small—and who better to take care of us? You are like family and we all need you, especially now." She smiled and rubbed her bulging belly.

Maggie squeezed her hand and smiled, acknowledging acceptance of the role, but still uncertain she was equal to the task.

"Get changed and I'll show you the house," Caroline said, giddy with excitement. "Remember when we thought Donegal Hall was something to see? This home is simply unbelievable."

Caroline left Maggie to unpack and dress. After so many shocks, Maggie didn't know if she could take any more in one day. But her curiosity got the best of her. She was dying to see the rest of the home.

She walked through the kitchen and butler's pantry to the large dining room. Carved wooden fireplace mantels adorned the walls with sparkling gas Baccarat crystal chandeliers glistening above an enormous Queen Anne mahogany table fit for a king. Twenty blue damask wooden chairs with matching draperies against the floor-to-ceiling windows painted a picture in Maggie's head of fine society dinners.

As she passed into the main salon, she stared up in amazement at the soaring ceilings above her and the surrounding walls covered with wood on the squared wainscoting. The equally towering windows, cased with wide carved wood trim, streamed great beams of sunlight on the inlaid wood floors.

"Isn't this place marvelous?" Caroline bragged with enthusiasm. "Can you believe this is our home?"

Caroline toured Maggie through each and every one of the remaining ten rooms in the apartment, including their bedrooms and guest rooms, the marbled water closets, and the library with soaring bookcases lined with volumes of books.

"I think there's a whole forest full of wood in this house," Caroline laughed. "And the marble gleams so, you can nearly see your image in it. Moira just loves the nursery and so will the baby. Bryne really thought of everything to make us so comfortable and happy here."

"Sorry there's a lot to do. The trunks are in the rooms. I'm so overwhelmed and can't seem to catch my breath," she said.

Maggie looked at Caroline's peaked skin and told her to lie down for a while, so she could get to work. She put Moira down for a nap while she unpacked all the family's trunks and suitcases, filled with their clothing and belongings, then turned to the dining room to unload the crates of linens, silver, china, and crystal—all unused since the wedding.

At the end of the day, she got Caroline and Moira ready for sleep and collapsed in her bed, exhausted by the work she had completed and daunted by the tasks ahead, including staffing the house with maids and a nanny. Easily closing her tired eyes, she drifted off dreaming of the adventures to come.

Awakening for the new day, she smelled delightful aromas wafting from the nearby kitchen and entered to find Mrs. Carmichael hard at work cooking breakfast.

"Mr. Gordan said he will serve, but I assume you'll be setting the table for their breakfast," Mrs. Carmichael said as a matter of fact.

Mrs. Carmichael was a small round woman around Mr. Gordan's age with graying blonde hair. Maggie instantly detected a tiny brogue here and there in her speech, but wasn't sure she was a kin of the isle.

"It's a pleasure to meet you, Mrs. Carmichael. Everything smells glorious. I can see you're a skilled cook. If you don't mind my asking, which part of Ireland are ya from?" Maggie gently inquired.

"Hah!" she said without lifting her head and hands from her busy work. "That's a fine thing. Me ma was from County Cork, but I was born here."

"Oh, I apologize for my blunder. I thought Mr. Gordan said ya were an Irish cook," Maggie said.

"I said me ma was Irish, didn't I?" she retorted, never missing a step of her work. "Now, the table?"

"I can set it for the viscount, but the viscountess takes a tray in her room for breakfast," Maggie said.

Mrs. Carmichael stopped what she was doing cold and stared at Maggie with daggers in her eyes.

"I was told to prepare an American breakfast for this household. In America, the master and mistress eat in the dining room with proper service every morning," she said firmly.

Maggie nodded and scooted into the dining room, quickly set the table for Bryne and Caroline. Then she trotted over to Caroline's room to awaken and dress her.

"No tray?" Caroline asked, bemused.

"I'm told in America the mister and mistress of the house to eat the morning meal in the dining room," Maggie said succinctly while gathering clothes for the day.

After she finished dressing Caroline, she went to Moira's room to awaken and feed her some porridge and milk Mrs. Carmichael brought on a tray.

"I'm not making a habit of delivering trays. Just for now, mind you. Until you engage a regular staff. I'm the cook; I don't serve," she warned Maggie and handed her the tray.

Since the household was small, Mr. Gordan agreed to act as Bryne's valet and perform regular meal service for small occasions. Footmen could be hired for entertaining. Maggie would still be Caroline's lady's maid, but with the baby coming, she knew she needed to employ more staff right away. Until then, she would have to do everything.

Running a household was all a bit intimidating, but luckily she always paid careful attention to Gallagher, Mrs. Doyle and her mother Windermere, during her lifetime of service. And with her culmination of knowledge, she believed there would be some pebbles in the road, but she was not solely unprepared for the position. She was beginning to think she was ready to become Mrs. Donnelly.

In the light of the new day, Maggie walked about the home, looking at it with new eyes. Instead of opulence and grandeur that amazed her mere hours ago, she now saw it through Mrs. Donnelly's clear Irish eyes—and the reality of the work to maintain such a grand home. Now she saw giant windows and floors to be cleaned, furniture to be polished and a forest of wood, as Caroline accurately quipped, to be dusted. Plus, three water closets to shine.

Then there was coal and wood to be brought up from the street level and fireplaces to be swept out every day. Lamps to light and diffuse. And linens to cart up to the 8th and 9th floors to launder. Even with a small household, there was a lot to do.

Thankfully, Mrs. Carmichael agreed to tidy the kitchen and act as scullery maid "when there were fewer dishes," she stated with utmost clarity and Mr. Gordan begrudgingly agreed to lite and extinguish the lights every day.

Figuring the hours and daily tasks, Maggie decided to begin with two young maids who she could teach and mold to her style. She remembered when she began service at Windermere under her mother's tutelage at thirteen years of age, Katherine taught her the proper way to run an Irish home.

Thinking of her mother's lessons made her tear a little, missing home. But with no time to waste, she needed help immediately to avoid working to an early grave.

"Mr. Gordan, where might I go to find some young Irish maids to engage for service?" Maggie asked.

She specifically settled on Irish maids, so they would speak the same language and understand the old country ways. With an American butler and cook, she needed the comfort of her own team who would not look down on her as an immigrant, foreign to American practices.

Before he could answer, Mrs. Carmichael said Mrs. O'Malley, a maid in the building, had two young daughters, Molly and Mary, who were able to begin service duties. The girls were thirteen and fourteen years of age.

"Brilliant. Can I see them right now?" Maggie asked.

"Fine. I'll make the introduction and you can speak to Mrs. O'Malley," she said.

Maggie followed Mrs. Carmichael up the stairs to the eighth-floor laundry room. It was dark and hot, filled with steam from the hot irons and scrub bins.

"Mrs. O'Malley, I'll introduce you to Mrs. Donnelly. She's looking for two young Irish maids to staff. Now I'll take my leave before I melt into a pool," Mrs. Carmichael said and hastily exited.

Mrs. O'Malley's appearance was indicative of the room—her apron and dress were soaked in sweat and dirt from the work and heat. Her mop cap dripped beads of water onto her orange hair.

"I wish I could meet ya in a better place in keeping with your position, mum, but I'm in here all day," Mrs. O'Malley said.

"Make no apologies for hard work, Mrs. O'Malley. What county do your people lay?" Maggie asked kindly.

"We're from County Cork, just like Mrs. Carmichael's mother. I know it's not right for a maid to be a mother, but when my husband died and we lost our farm, this was the best I could do. Me daughters are young, but they cared for the house while I helped on the farm and will work hard and mind ya," she said earnestly. "They're staying with me brother now cause I've no way to house them here. I send money to feed them though."

"Me mother back in County Donegal taught me by her side too, so I'm sure as heaven they learned well." Maggie put her hand on Mrs. O'Malley's shoulder.

"Please send them to me tomorrow morning and ya can all live here in the quarters together," Maggie said and went back to the apartment.

"Mr. Gordan, the two young maids will begin tomorrow, but I still need a nanny. We prefer an Irish woman, but she could be English too, but not Scottish. We need to be able to understand each other and don't want the littlens to pick up any improper speech," she instructed.

"Excellent. I will place an advertisement in the paper today," Gordon said.

"Thank you. The viscountess and I can begin interviews immediately," she said.

Dearest Mother,

We arrived in America and are nearly set up. It's an odd place, it is, but wonderful too. The buildings are something to see—big and tall enough to touch St. Peter himself. They even have a big stone lady standing there in the water to welcome you. Strange thing.

And there are so many people from different places, it's a wonder anyone knows what each other is saying. But it surely gives me some comfort that I'm not the only one from somewhere else.

Our place is grand indeed. That much the mister got right. I'll bet me buttons that he used Caroline's dowry for it, unless the railroad is giving it to him. I know you'd say it's not for me to think of, but it just burns my bottom the way he treats Caroline and everyone like his personal puppets.

I hired two young Irish girls for maids. They're doing fine. Both are good listeners and hard workers, but I need to keep an eye on them.

The other day, I saw Bryne watching Molly, a pretty blonde girl with pale skin and blue eyes. She's petite and for a lass of thirteen, she has quite a figure, but she's an innocent babe. His eyes were locked on her and I saw a devilish leer on his face. She's just his type. But then again, I'm beginning to think any female is his type.

We don't see a lot of him at home since the move. Except for breakfasts and dinner a few times a week, he's off at his new office or at his fancy men's club.

Suzanne Rudd Hamilton

I can tell it bothers Carrie a little. She keeps saying he's busy starting his new job with the railroad and making important connections. But I'll tell you, every time I look at the man, I see the devil himself. I know you'd say that's my Irish temperament seeing things through my green eyes, but if you'll pardon my poisoned thoughts about the man, I think he's on the hunt again for what he can't get at home with Carrie in the family way again.

She's having an awful time with this one. I think the move and the voyage were too much for her delicate condition. She's sick nearly every morning and very weak. She mostly just lies around and crochets for the new baby.

Although Bryne did make me a present of a brand-new sewing machine. You should see her, ma—she makes the stitching go faster than a bolt of lightning. Me poor bruised purple fingers are thanking him for that.

I'm making some things for the new baby. We're hoping for a boy this time—Carrie and me are, and Bryne.

I'll write soon. I'm missing you and home something terrible.

Your darling daughter,

Maggie.

Irish Eyes

Suzanne Rudd Hamilton

Chapter Eight

No Irish nannies responded to the advertisement, but several young American girls and one English lady inquired. Since Caroline was too sick to interview the candidates, she left the hiring in Maggie's hands.

"The viscountess is unwell, so I will see the ladies," Maggie told Mr. Gordon.

Maggie saw one young American girl after another. Some were new to the city, while others were from New York families and wanted to help their family income. They were peppy, pretty, sweet and dainty. But all Maggie could see was more places for Bryne's eye to stray and potential victims she'd have to protect.

Then Mrs. Bingham came in. She was an older English woman with a tall imposing figure and a strict, no-nonsense disposition. Dressed in black head to toe with umbrella and purse in hand, she entered and brazenly walked around the sitting room, carefully examining it from top to bottom, nodding her head.

"Acceptable so far," she said and firmly sat down in the chair.

"I'm Mrs. Donnelly and I'll be asking ya a few questions." Maggie was stunned at the woman's blunt demeanor, but as she was definitely not Bryne's type, she pressed on.

"The correct English is to say 'I would like to ask you a few questions' or 'I would like to make inquiries of you,'" she retorted in a matter-of-fact and slightly annoyed voice and placed some papers on the table.

"Let me save you the trouble. I've been a nanny for thirty years. First for Lord and Lady Albany and then for Lord and Lady Breckenridge. Here are my impeccable references. I have my own apartment. Is that all?"

Maggie took the papers off the table and quickly reviewed them, peering above the papers to as Mrs. Bingham impatiently tapped her umbrella in perfect cadence on the wood floor.

"Thank you, these seem in order. We have a toddler girl and the baby will be here shortly," Maggie said.

"I'm not a wet nurse, but I do like babies. I get to start from a blank slate with no bad habits. I hope the girl didn't pick up any unseemly behavior," Mrs. Bingham said.

"Oh, no, Moira is a beautiful wisp of a girl. Sweet and pure as a sprite," Maggie smiled with pride.

"I'll be the judge of that. I'll see the nursery now," she ordered and promptly stood up.

Confused, Maggie led her into the nursery where Moira was napping. She slowly opened the door halfway and stepped out of the way so Mrs. Bingham could see.

Suzanne Rudd Hamilton

The woman looked in for a second and then turned around quickly like a soldier and promptly walked down the hallway.

Maggie quietly closed the door and quickly stepped after her to the entrance, when they both stopped just short of the door.

"I will take the position. Start immediately. There is no time to spare," she said and exited before Maggie knew what happened.

She closed the door and walked toward the salon, reviewing the entire exchange in her mind, shaking her head when Caroline entered.

"I thought I heard someone in the nursery. Do we have a new nanny?" she asked.

"Well, I'm not sure if we have a new nanny or if she has us, but either way the position has been filled," Maggie chuckled.

"Thank you, Maggie. I know you always have our best in mind," she said and sat down in her chair to crochet. "Please send some tea in."

Maggie went into the kitchen, still reeling from the interaction with Mrs. Bingham, and asked Mr. Gordon to bring tea to the viscountess while she tended to the nursery.

"I would expect an English nanny to be a very proper addition indeed," he said and left with the tea service.

Maggie walked to the nursery, silently debating her choice, as she woke Moira for her afternoon constitutional. Every day she strolled with Moira in an open pram through the grassed area across from The Dakota called Central Park.

Maggie let Moira run in the grass and they sang songs and played games. While it wasn't the emerald hills of Ireland, it reminded Maggie of the vast acres at Windermere where she and Caroline played. It gave them both a chance to breathe some fresh air.

She reflected on the household changes. Only she and Caroline raised Moira so far, so she was a little hesitant to introduce another person to the young tot. Maggie thought of Moira as her own and wanted her to know the old country ways and not forget where she came from. But with the new baby, she couldn't keep up the house and mind the children too. Mrs. Bingham was an unfortunate necessity and would be an adjustment for all.

As she laid Moira down for bed that night, she told her favorite harboo tales of Tír na nÓg. When she fell to sleep, Maggie watched the sweet babe for a few minutes and a tear streamed down her cheek. With an English nanny in charge, she wondered if this was the last time Moira would hear the beloved Irish story.

The next morning was busy with introductions and orienting Mrs. Bingham. After visiting the kitchen, Maggie presented her to Bryne and Caroline.

Caroline mustered a friendly hello and rose to shake her hand, but Bryne barely lifted his newspaper to greet the new nanny.

After she and Caroline walked Mrs. Bingham to the nursery, Maggie went back into the dining room and saw Bryne ogling Molly, touching her backside as she took away the breakfast plates.

"Molly, I'll take these," Maggie interrupted. "Mind the dishes."

Bryne glared at Maggie for her interference.

"I see you found the oldest and ugliest nanny in New York," he chuckled.

Maggie took a deep breath and fired her green eyes at him, but uttered all she could express in a pleasant tone.

"She's English," she said, took several plates and left the room. Once out of earshot, she muttered. "Not another lamb for ya to slaughter."

After a few weeks, Mrs. Bingham was sweet to Moira, but making no friends with the other staff.

"She thinks she's the Queen of England, asking for her tea brought to her in a certain way. I'll spike her tea with some Irish if she pushes too hard with her fine English airs," Mrs. Carmichael warned Maggie.

"I will discuss the household schedule with her, but please try to be patient. The baby's coming soon, and we need her," Maggie explained.

As Maggie went to the nursery, she heard a moaning coming from Caroline's room. She rushed to open the door to find Caroline on the floor.

"I don't know what's going on. Something's wrong," Caroline said, frightened.

Maggie ran down the hallway and asked Mr. Gordon to quickly get a doctor, told Mrs. Carmichael to boil water, and shouted at the girls to follow her with the pantry rags and drying towels. Then she soaked some towels with cold water and ran back to Caroline. With the girls' help, she lifted Caroline into bed. Maggie told them to go, as she didn't want them to be scared by Caroline's loud moans and fast-paced breathing.

Maggie sat with Caroline's head on her lap, soothing her with the cold compress, stroking her hair and telling her everything was fine. But she wasn't sure. Her birthing experience was limited to Moira's bearing, as she stood by and helped the doctor, and watching a few farm animals deliver. This was very different.

As Caroline calmed herself, Maggie changed her into a nightdress and got everything ready for the birth. Just as she finished, Caroline shrieked in pain.

"I feel as if a knife is plunging into my belly," she cried.

Maggie knew she had to look and see if the baby was coming out sooner than expected. She laid Caroline on her back and looked through her legs. She could see the opening widen and saw the top of the baby's head.

Taking a deep breath, she made a sign of the cross to pray for help.

"The baby's coming, Carrie. I don't know if we can wait for the doctor. We're going to do this together. I need ya to sit up, hold onto the bedpost and push hard when I tell you," Maggie ordered in a calm and peaceful tone so Caroline wouldn't be scared and moved her to the corner of the bed.

"I feel the devil inside!" Caroline yelled.

"We'll be fine." Maggie spoke to her in an easy tone, but was secretly terrified. She feared for the life of both Caroline and her baby, but knew she had to do something.

Caroline screamed as she bore down and pushed, gritting her teeth. But the baby didn't come.

"I need ya to push like the devil himself is after ya, Carrie," Maggie said in a little more confident and urgent voice.

Caroline held tighter to the post and screamed louder. Her face turned bright red as she pushed harder.

The baby was not coming out. Maggie wanted to panic, but knew she needed to keep her composure, or she'd lose them both. She looked around and listened for the doctor, but heard nothing. She kept hoping the doctor would rush in and take charge, but he hadn't arrived. It was up to her.

She told Caroline to rest for a second and she gently put her fingers around the opening to see if she could coax the head out a little. She lightly pressed on the edges and saw the head pop out a little. Encouraged, she massaged them again and saw it emerge a little more.

"That's it," she said, smiling at Caroline. "This is going to work, but I need ya to give it all ya have deep inside. Push against the footboard to give yourself a boost and hold onto that post and the wee babe will come."

Caroline took a deep breath and bore down screaming so loud, Maggie thought the windows would crack. Maggie placed her fingers around the opening and pressed, then softly pulled a little as the baby's head started to come out.

"Come on, Carrie, don't let the devil beat ya, push harder!" Maggie cheered as Caroline pushed so hard her face turned dark red.

The baby finally came out in one swift movement like riding down a slide. Maggie grabbed the babe but noticed it wasn't crying or moving. She told Caroline to rest as she placed it in the warm towels. The baby's color was a slight tinge of purple and it wasn't breathing.

Worried, but thinking quickly, Maggie separated the baby's lip and cleared his mouth with her fingers, then breathed into the baby's mouth once, then twice. Nothing. She tried again, this time pressing her lips against the babe's and blowing her life into its body.

"It worked!" she exclaimed as the baby let out a big wailing cry. "It's a boy!"

Caroline lay on the bed pale and weak from exhaustion, but smiled a bit.

"No wonder he didn't want to come out," Maggie laughed with tears streaming down. "He has a big ball of a head, like a pumpkin."

Just as Maggie started to clean the baby off, the doctor arrived. She explained everything that happened, and he examined the baby and then Caroline and cut the umbilical cord. But as soon as he cut the cord, Caroline began to moan again and started to bleed.

"Give the baby to someone; I'm going to need your help," he said sternly.

Maggie ran into the hallway and called for Mrs. Bingham. She handed the boy to her and told her to keep him warm. Then she ran back into Caroline's room.

"I need your help. Hold her hands and get her to bear down again," he said urgently.

"But she's so weak," Maggie said, scared, looking down at Caroline's fragile body and propping it up on her chest, then clasping both her hands.

"I know you've spent your last, but I need ya to give me more, Carrie," Maggie softly spoke into her ear.

"I can't," Caroline said, barely audible, with her head bobbing slightly.

"Yes, ya can," Maggie ordered. "You're not leaving me alone with two littlens and Bryne. Fight!"

Maggie yelled and pushed on Caroline's lower back to help her bear down, squeezing her hand.

Caroline let out a weakened yelp and pushed a little.

"Again!" the doctor commanded.

Maggie pushed against Caroline's body and squeezed her hand tighter. Weakened past exhaustion, Caroline pushed a little and exhaled an enormous sigh.

"Good," the doctor said pulling out the broken pieces of placenta. "Now let her rest."

Maggie laid Caroline on a bed of pillows, put more wet compresses on her head, covered her in blankets, and kissed her on the forehead.

"No one could've done better. You're the grandest mother in the world," Maggie whispered to her.

She pulled the doctor to the corner of the room so Caroline wouldn't hear.

"Will she be fine?" Maggie asked, afraid of the answer.

"I believe so. She lost some blood, but with rest, she should recover," the doctor said and squeezed Maggie's arm. "You saved both their lives."

Maggie went to the kitchen to tell the staff of the baby's arrival. She instructed Mrs. Carmichael to make some hearty chicken broth for Caroline and directed Mr. Gordon to let her know when the viscount returned. Then she told Mary to watch Moira for Mrs. Bingham.

She needed to get back to Caroline, but she quickly went into the nursery to check on the boy. Mrs. Bingham cleaned him, dressed him in his layette and set him in his bassinet, swaddled in the blanket Maggie embroidered.

"The doctor says he's fine, but keep a close eye on him. He was born without breath," Maggie explained. "Mary can watch Moira."

As she entered Caroline's room, Maggie felt scared seeing her drained and limp body lying there in the bed. She was peaceful and alive, but when the doctor left, Maggie vowed not to leave her side.

She sat beside Caroline in bed, applying new wet compresses and stroking her hair, while feeding her water and broth.

Caroline glimmered a small smile as she felt Maggie's hand on her head.

"Should we call him Kieran or Conner?" she softly uttered.

"Kieran is a good Irish name. Now rest," Maggie smiled.

Irish Eyes

Chapter Nine

Late in the evening, Mr. Gordon popped his head in and told her the viscount had returned. Maggie asked the butler to stay and watch over the sleeping Caroline for a few minutes.

Looking in the sitting room and dining room, she couldn't find Bryne. She knocked on his bedroom door, but no answer. Then she walked over to the library and smelled the scent of his cigar. She opened the door and found him pinning Molly against the bookcase with the weight of his body, ravenously kissing her neck and fondling her bosom.

"So this is what I find ya doing as your wife lay with only the angels to keep her alive!" Maggie yelled, interrupting them.

He turned around and chuckled, while a frightened Molly ran out of the room.

"You forget yourself, woman." Bryne sat down in his chair, picking up his cigar and his drink. "I am the master of this house."

Maggie looked at him with ire and disgust welling up in her green eyes.

"I'll have ya know that while your sorry self was taking your jollies from every girl who meets your fancy, your poor wife nearly met her maker today giving ya a son!" she yelled.

Bryne sat up straight and smiled. "A son?"

"Yes, the saints were smiling on you, as now ya have your precious heir, but only by the Lord's good graces has Kieran come to us and spared his angelic mother. Not that ya deserve her, him, or that sweet pixie of a daughter either," Maggie said, sternly shaking her finger at him.

"Kieran. No, that won't do. My son is born an American and requires a strong American name. William. William Donegal." Bryne declared, disregarded everything she said and charged out of the room, leaving Maggie to run behind him.

"You'll be kind to her now. She's still in a weak state," Maggie warned. Bryne ignored her and marched to the nursery, opening the door.

"Where is my son? I want to see William," he ordered Mrs. Bingham.

She pointed to the baby in the bassinet next to her and stepped away.

Maggie pulled Mrs. Bingham to the side. "Watch him," she said, exiting the nursery in a huff.

She took a few deep breaths, closed her eyes, and counted to three to quell her temper before entering Caroline's room. She wasn't going to divulge anything that happened or tell her how high and mighty Bryne changed the baby's name. Caroline needed complete rest and peace to recuperate. Maggie would not have her upset.

After Mr. Gordon left, Maggie sat up next to Caroline, changing her compress again and gently drying her forehead.

"Did you tell Bryne about Kieran?" she asked in a faint voice.

"I did. Now go back to sleep and dream wonderful thoughts of your sweet babes," Maggie said in a soft voice. She hummed her an old Irish song to lull her back to sleep.

Maggie sat next to her all night, seething with anger at the sight of Bryne taking advantage of Molly, while his wife lay so ill. And then he didn't even care to see her, only his son and heir.

Finally ebbing to sleep, she happily dreamed of Bryne being poked by the devil engulfed in flames for his misdeeds.

"Mrs. Donnelly," Mr. Gordon said, abruptly waking her.

"Mrs. Carmichael wants to know if she should make a tray for the viscountess."

"Just tea and toast, thank you," Maggie said, shaking herself awake.

She took off the compresses and dried Caroline's head as her friend slowly yawned into consciousness.

Caroline raised her head with a little smile and a bit of pink color in her cheeks.

Two days later, Caroline was sitting up with nearly all the color back in her eyes as she held and fed the baby boy, grinning at her small miracle.

When she was done, Mrs. Bingham took the baby but pulled Maggie aside.

"Mrs. Donnelly, I really must object. The viscountess should not nurse her own child. A woman of her station is not an animal; we must engage a wet nurse."

Maggie lifted her chin and looked at Mrs. Bingham straight in the eyes with a superior glance.

"My dear Mrs. Bingham, the Irish take care of their own," she declared and walked away.

In the evening, Caroline was feeling much better. Maggie barely left her side, but now that she was reasonably assured that Caroline was on the mend, she could return to her duties running the household.

Bryne burst into Caroline's room later in the evening happy as a lark, holding two boxes in his hands.

"I'll see my wife now," he declared and nodded to Maggie to leave.

She left the room and passed him, glaring disapproval at him with her green eyes glaring right through him.

"Did you see our boy, Bryne?" Caroline's eyes sparkled with pride.

"Yes, William is a fine boy—strong and healthy," Bryne said.

"No, silly, his name is Kieran," Caroline giggled.

"Don't worry about anything. I had my attorney complete all the paperwork. Our son is the first American in the family and he has a strong American name. William Bryne Donegal, the future 8th viscount."

Caroline looked down and rubbed her blanket between her fingers. "Whatever you feel is best, darling," she mumbled.

"Now, now, little bird, perk up." He sat down next to her, lifted her chin with his finger and kissed her on the forehead.

"Now that little William has been born, you can join your place in New York society," he smiled. "Every lady in town is brimming with excitement to have tea with the Viscountess of Donegal in their parlor."

"Really?" She looked up and smiled with an innocent sparkle.

"We already have invitations for some balls in a week or two with some influential families and you will be the queen." He smiled and placed a red velvet box with a big blue ribbon on it in front of her.

Caroline smiled and gleamed as her blue eyes sparkled with the excitement of a child at Christmas as she swiftly untied the ribbon and opened the velvet box. Inside was a beautiful gold tiara with three emeralds poised in the middle, surrounding a large diamond in the center, and small twinkling diamonds laced around the front.

Bryne took it out of the box and placed it on her head.

"For my Irish queen, a crown to capture your beauty for all to see." He grinned and kissed her on the cheek.

Caroline beamed and held her head up high with the magnificent jewel on her head, modeling it with pride.

"I'll leave you now to rest," Bryne said.

"Thank you so much for the gift. But oh, please stay, darling. I would enjoy your company," she said hopefully.

"I would love to, my dearest, but I have an early appointment, so I must retire. And you need to rest, so you can soon stroll on my arm to outshine every woman in New York," he smiled.

Maggie returned with some warm milk for Caroline to sleep and saw her pretending she was at a ball, miming and waving her hand to the invisible attendees.

"Thank you, Mrs. Astor; I am pleased to make your acquaintance," Caroline said.

"Looks like the Leprechauns visited you. That crown shimmers more than the stars in the sky and a pot o' gold put together," Maggie remarked.

"Isn't it the grandest thing you've ever seen?" Caroline grinned. "Maggie, I was wrong about Bryne. Now that William's born, he's going to take me to balls and show me the wonderful New York society life. Things are going to be fine."

"William?" Maggie asked, confused.

"Yes," Caroline said, placing the tiara in the box. "Since he's an American, Bryne says he needs an American name, not an Irish one. "You'll make me a new ballgown to go with this magnificent tiara, won't you, Maggie?" she asked, handing Maggie the box.

"Of course." Maggie gritted her teeth. "I've had my eye on some green fabric. You'll be the gem of the Emerald Isle."

Maggie put the tiara away in the bureau and walked out the door.

"I'll call him Liam, spite the father. American or not, an Irish lad deserves an Irish name."

As she walked past the library, she smelled cigar smoke and Bryne called to her.

"Maggie, please come in."

She walked up to his chair and he handed her a small red velvet box wrapped in a blue ribbon.

"Caroline wanted you to have this for everything you do for her and the children," he said. "She said your mother has one just like it."

Maggie curiously removed the ribbon and opened the box. Inside was a dainty onyx cameo with an ivory and gold relief of a woman, similar to the one her mother always wore on her collar.

"This family owes you a debt of gratitude. Without you, I would not have William or maybe even Caroline. You have my considerable respect and appreciation," he said and pinned the cameo to her collar.

Despite her usual disdain, Maggie was disarmed by the gesture and left the room with a warm feeling. It was obvious he had someone else pick up the cameo and Caroline must have mentioned it before, but the gift was heartfelt. As she looked into his eyes, she saw how grateful he was. Maybe he was turning a new leaf. Maybe it would all be fine from now on.

Suzanne Rudd Hamilton

Chapter Ten

Finally out of bed, Caroline was anxious to begin her new life in New York society. After spending her first few months in America cloistered in the house, she was giddy with the anticipation of joining Bryne's side at the lavish outings of the elite.

For the first step, Bryne decided to have the head of the railroad, Mr. Milford and his wife to dinner.

Since his arrival in America, Bryne made a name for himself in his brief tenure at the Milford Western Railroad Company and garnered the attention of its founder.

His wife, Mrs. Elmira Gates Milford, was a prominent figure in the upper crust, as she came from an old money family who claimed to have developed roots in the city over two hundred years.

Caroline fussed around in a lather, bothering the staff all day to ensure everything was perfect for their first visitors in America.

"Mrs. Carmichael, we need a real American meal for our guests. Only the best," Caroline said, hovering over the cook.

"Yes, Viscountess, it's all taken care of," answered Mrs. Carmichael with a slight annoyance in her voice.

Caroline next cornered Molly and Mary. "Oh, and girls, make sure all the silver is polished and all the linens are ironed and spotless."

"And Gordon, let's go over the service tonight." Caroline began when Maggie interrupted.

"Viscountess, I need your decision on the selection of dress tonight," Maggie said and followed her back to her room.

"Carrie, you're going to work yourself to death with worry," Maggie said earnestly. "Do you trust me to make sure the dinner will go on well?"

Caroline looked at Maggie, smiled, and sighed in relief.

"Of course."

Maggie left her and went to the kitchen to oversee preparations for the dinner.

"I know ya will do the best job. As me mother used to say, you'll never plough a field by turning it over in your mind. Please forgive the viscountess. Tonight is important to her," she said.

Everyone smiled at Maggie and continued with their work.

Caroline was a bundle of nerves when Maggie dressed her for dinner. She fidgeted about like never before, refixing her hair, re-buttoning her collar and changing her earbobs twice. She needed a distraction to quiet her stress.

"I wanted to thank ya so much for the cameo, Carrie," Maggie said, touching the cameo on her collar. "I know it really came from you. It was so considerate."

"It sure looks grand on you," Caroline beamed, then grimaced with frustration. "I mean, it looks marvelous. Bryne told me to watch my Irish country words in front of New York people. I need to try to speak like an American."

Maggie frowned at the idea of losing her identity but decided to save a conversation about that remark for another time. Caroline had enough on her mind.

Bryne returned home and changed just in time for the Milfords to arrive.

Mr. and Mrs. Milford were in their early 50s, both with temples of gray showing beneath their hats.

Mrs. Milford was petite in stature with a pinkish face and apple cheeks. She smiled and spoke very fast with a sweet girlish giggle. It sounded like the trill of friendly birdsong.

Mr. Milford was unusually short for a man, at a few inches taller than his wife, but he stood remarkably upright. He wore a monocle, which he often held with his fingers.

Bryne greeted them and introduced Caroline.

"My dear, you are a beautiful Irish rose," Mrs. Milford said. "I will enjoy launching you into our world."

Her words put Caroline immediately at ease, knowing she had a friendly guide.

"Yes, we love the Irish. They are the foundation of the Union Pacific Railroad. There's an Irishman buried under every tie on that track." Mr. Milford laughed and quickly stopped once he saw the astonished blank stares around him, rejecting his inappropriate humor.

At dinner, Mrs. Milford dominated the conversation with gossip about upcoming parties and the people who would attend.

Mr. Milford said very little and cleared his throat a lot. While she spoke, he barely stopped eating, emitting a chuckle here and there at her indiscreet tales of this one or that one. She was funny and whimsical.

Caroline was in a whirlwind following her rapid conversation, trying to drink in every word.

Since Gordon reported the guests were just beginning dessert, Maggie looked in on Moira and Liam to tell them a story and give Mrs. Bingham a moment to herself. The care of a new babe made the nanny a little more amenable to Maggie's involvement with the children for stories or walks, since they afforded her time for tea or brief rests.

Little Liam was a sweet cherub, as Maggie called him, because of his round face and head and rosy plump cheeks. He was a happy baby, cooing and gurgling in his bassinet.

After she told the children nighttime Irish tales, despite Mrs. Bingham's rolling eyes, she went back to the kitchen to check on the dishes.

As she passed the dining room, she heard Mrs. Milford rattling on to Caroline about Mrs. Astor's upcoming New Year's ball. She assumed the men were in the library for cigars and brandy, since she didn't hear their voices. She suddenly remembered some special candies she found while shopping for an after-dinner treat.

The kitchen was pretty quiet as Mary was finishing the last of the dishes.

As she opened the door to the walk-in pantry, she saw Bryne pressing his weight against Molly, kissing her on the mouth with his hands up her skirt.

She immediately closed the door in reflex, embarrassed and stunned by what she had witnessed, and stood there for a few seconds, unsure of her next move.

Bryne came out right away and shot her an arrogant, satisfied glare as he walked back to the library to join Mr. Milford.

"Have some brandy sent to the library. I found my special cigars," he said in a snide tone, carrying a wooden cigar box.

Maggie pursed her lips and charged into the pantry to talk to Molly. The girl looked worried at Maggie's stern face, but not frightened by what she experienced.

"I'm only going to ask once," Maggie scolded, trying to hold back her ire. "Are ya willing with the mister or is he taking advantage?"

Molly looked down at the floor to avoid the intense gaze of Maggie's green eyes.

"I don't know," she blurted, scared and unsure by her innocence and inexperience.

Maggie shook her head. Molly was so young and easily vulnerable to a man's attentions; she just sighed and let her go.

"On with ya then," she said.

Forgetting the after-dinner candies, Maggie went to her room to calm herself and think of what to do. Should she dismiss her and hire an ugly maid? Should she talk to the girl's mother? Should she talk to Caroline?

Maggie was mixed up with all the questions swirling in her head, while still fuming at Bryne for putting them all in such a position.

"Mrs. Donnelly?" Mary asked softly, standing in the doorway with her head down.

"Yes, Mary," Maggie said, taking a deep breath.

"Please don't dismiss my sister. She doesn't know what she's doing," she begged.

Maggie waved her into the room and pointed to the chair.

"Mary, is the mister forcing himself on her?" Maggie asked.

"At first, his attentions made her giddy. That the master himself would be pleased with the likes of her. But I think he means to rob her virtue and I'm afeared for her."

"Thank ya for telling me, Mary. She's an innocent lamb. I will see what I can do. Now upstairs with both of ya and go on to sleep."

Mary left and Maggie sat on her bed, pensively debating in her mind.

She couldn't reprimand Molly and dismissing her would be unfair punishment just for being pretty. She can't help that.

If she talked to Mrs. O'Malley, it may shame the girl. And if she told Caroline, she may not believe her and besides, there was little she could do. It seemed everything would make it worse. But she couldn't abide the poor girl being harmed. It was all Bryne's fault.

She knew from the beginning he had a wandering eye with an insatiable appetite for women, but she never said anything to upset Caroline.

When Gordon came back and notified her the Milfords were gone, Maggie went to Caroline's room to ready her for bed, not knowing if she would or could hold her tongue.

"It was a glorious evening," Caroline said happily, humming. "Mrs. Milford is a craic and she's going to show me around. I can't wait to go to the balls and parties. Bryne will take me in his arms and dance with me, just like when we first met. He'll look deeply into my eyes and they will only be for me. He said he's going to visit me tonight."

She was giggling and prancing around the room. Maggie couldn't tell her. She hoped this new chapter in their marriage would diminish his extracurricular activities and maybe he would leave poor Molly alone.

When she went back to her room, she knew there was nothing left to do. She wrote to her mother.

Dearest Mother,

Moira and the new babe, Liam, are the joys of me life. Little Liam is such a doll. I wish you could see him. I tell them tales of the old country every night, like you told me when I was a babe. Their father doesn't want them to know our ways, but I won't let them forget. To be sure, I'm sewing them a pillow embroidered with an old Irish yarn.

Carrie is better now and itching to spread her wings in New York. She's has so many invitations for teas and lunches, more than when she was courting back home. She's going to have a dandy time. But that bastard of a husband of hers, him and his roving eyes... and hands. That one, he's always grabbing, poking and pinching any skirt that passes him by. But this time he went too far. Poor

Suzanne Rudd Hamilton

little Molly O'Malley. A mere girl, only thirteen in years and I put her right in the lion's den, I did.

I've caught the slimy bastard up against her several times. She's too young to understand he's the devil.

I'm afraid for her. The nerve he has to compromise young girls and lord over his position, the wicked dark soul.

Caroline must know of his devilish ways, true to heart. He spends many nights away from home until late. There's nothing she can do, but she's dreaming hearts and flowers now, since he lays with her again. But to him, it's just another meal. That one suffers from a double dose of original sin, he does.

I'm outta my head with worry, Ma. I keep thinking of everything you told me and praying for an answer. I'll light another candle in church.

Like you say, a good laugh and a good sleep will cure any woe. I will lay me head down and hope the light will shine a new day on me.

Your darling Maggie

Chapter Eleven

Caroline's days were bustling between the steady stream of society mavens calling at the house and the parties, teas, lunches and meetings. Mrs. Milford wore her heels out showing off her new protégé, the Viscountess of Donegal.

Given she used Caroline's title at her whim, Maggie thought Mr. Milford enjoyed the prestige of having an Irish aristocrat as her pupil from across the pond.

She's nearly transformed Caroline's speech, habits and demeanor into a true American socialite.

Bryne puffed his chest with pride having the belle of New York on his arm for every party, lavishing her with baubles, attention and praise and filling her head with romantic gestures and deeds every night.

Maggie worked on the dress for Mrs. Astor's ball for weeks. When she pushed the littlens in the pram around the block and in the park, she watched the fine ladies and looked in the shop windows for ideas. And the new sewing machine pushed her to try new techniques in stitching that she had never dreamed possible.

With the special green and gold shiny fabric, Maggie created a beautiful ballgown with a full hooped skirt from the cinched waist and puffy off-the-shoulder sleeves with a sweetheart neckline. Unlike the fancy dresses she made before, this was a gown for a viscountess. The crowning touch was the tiara Bryne gave her after Liam's birth.

"Maggie, this is the most elegant dress you have ever made." Caroline beamed and twirled around. "I feel like the queen herself."

Bryne smiled, standing at the door looking in on her.

"That is a beautiful viscountess." He smiled, came in the room, and kissed Caroline on the cheek. "Close your eyes."

She giggled with anticipation as he opened a red velvet box he was hiding behind his back. He took out a heavy gold embossed necklace from the box and placed it around her neck. It glimmered against her alabaster skin with an emerald teardrop dropped right above her cleavage.

Caroline opened her eyes and gasped at the jewels.

"It pales next to your beauty, my dear." He smiled and kissed her hand.

Maggie was happy for Caroline, but she could barely stomach the false sweet sentiments coming out of his mouth.

"Smooth talk from an evil heart comes in sheep's clothing but really is a wolf," Maggie quipped to herself after they left.

She went back to her room to finish the embroidered pillow for the children's nursery with part of the chant Maggie and Carrie said to each other.

Wish, wish, shining star, make us be who we are, and if ye take us far from ours, keep us forever Anam Cara.

Suddenly she heard a wailing cry coming from the kitchen. She ran in to find Molly lying on the floor in the dark room howling in pain with Mary over her weeping with fear.

"What's wrong?" Maggie asked, fearing the worst.

"Missus, I think I killed her," Mary shouted.

Mary and Maggie picked Molly up from the floor, took her to Maggie's room and placed her on the bed. Molly was holding her stomach and shrieking with pain.

Maggie noticed a streak of blood trailing on the floor from the kitchen and took Mary to the side.

"What happened?" Maggie demanded.

"My fears came true. She's not bled in over a month and feels sick in the morning. I knew the mister ruined her," she cried. "We heard ya could drink borax and it would go away."

Molly let out a curdling yell and Mary screamed.

"She's dying. I killed my sister!" she cried.

"Go get your mother and bring her here now," Maggie commanded.

Mary ran out the door and up the back stairs, while Maggie put the kettle on and ran to the pantry to find the syrup of ipecac.

She forced Molly to drink it and she gagged it down. She helped the girl to the sink as she vomited, choking and crying in agony.

"Get the devil out, young lass," she said, wiping her brow.

Maggie took the kettle off and put some lemon and hot water in the cup, helped her drink a few sips and sat her in the chair.

With the girl calmer, Maggie held the cup to her mouth and told her to drink more.

When Mrs. O'Malley arrived with Mary, Maggie directed Mary to help her sister drink and explained everything to her mother.

"I think she'll be fine," Maggie told the girls' mother. "The poison should be out, but I don't know about the wee bairn."

"Saints be praised ya were here to help her," Mrs. O'Malley said, and she and Mary took Molly upstairs.

With the danger abated, Maggie started to fume like a volcano. With a full head of steam, she stomped out the door through the front entrance, down the elevator and out the main gate and crossed the street to the park.

It was well past midnight, so she encountered no one to scold her for using the resident and guest elevators and main entrance to the building.

The moon was bright, shining a beam through the darkness. She saw happy people skating without care on the iced ponds in Central Park. Once on the grass, she trudged back and forth, breathing smoke from the cold air and creating a path in her fury.

"A messenger of Satan, he is!" she yelled indiscriminately. "I saw his dastardly black coal soul. I fed the poor lass to the lion."

The steam coming from her head warmed the chill of the evening air from her as she clomped up and down the grass in a rage.

Usually, the feeling of the grass under her feet soothed her, like the rolling amber and green hills of her home. She tried closing her eyes and counting to three, but today, nothing would soothe her savage beast.

When she saw the Donegals' carriage pull up to the house, she took off in a tirade, following quickly behind in the elevator and threw open the front door of the apartment to find them laughing, with Bryne's hands on Caroline's shoulders.

"Take your hands off Carrie. Ya wolf, ya serpent of Satan. Ya take your leisures and plant your seed wherever ya want with no thought for your misdeeds or the souls ya harm in your wake!" she screamed with her face as red as hot flames.

"Maggie, have you lost your sense? You can't talk to the viscount that way," Caroline said, shocked.

"She was a babe and ya nearly killed her!" She walked up to Bryne and yelled right in his face, paying no attention to her friend's warning. "How many more are out there? How many lives can ya claim? How many births? Or just deaths?"

Bryne pushed her hard away from him, knocking her to the floor from the force.

"You're madder than a loon," Bryne said. "She has no idea what's she's saying."

Caroline stood in the middle of them, looking back and forth quickly in confusion and looked down at Maggie.

"I don't understand. What are you talking about?" Caroline shouted in panic.

"He had his way with our young maid Molly and gave her the family way. And she nearly died of poison trying to rid herself of it," Maggie accused, pointing at Bryne.

Caroline looked at Maggie with widened eyes in horror. She knew it was true. She'd known it for years.

"The girl is a liar. I don't touch lowly maids," he retorted.

"I caught ya many times holding your body against hers with your hand up her dress, cupping her bosom, forcing your mouth on hers. You're the liar! You're the devil himself!" Maggie roared with fire lit in her green eyes.

Huffing with anger, Bryne gazed with an icy stare, standing over Maggie still on the ground and slapped her hard across the face, sending her head to the floor. Then he stormed out the front door.

Neither Maggie nor Caroline uttered a sound. They stood in silence as Maggie slowly rose to her feet.

"The viscount is the master of this house and my husband," Caroline said softly clenching her teeth and wiping the tears streaming down her face, distraught and unnerved.

"Carrie, this is a long time coming. Ya knew of his ways. And ya know what me mother said. If ya lie down with dogs, you'll rise with fleas," Maggie warned angrily.

The sheen in the moon's beam glistened the tears wetting her whole face. She looked straight through Maggie with a blank stare as if she were nothing but a ghostly figure.

"You need to leave. For good," she said. She ran out of the room sobbing.

Maggie stood in the middle of the room in shock. This was it. The deepest of cuts. A breach of faith and trust. Their friendship. Their sisterhood. Despite everything they meant to each other and knowing the truth about Bryne. Caroline still chose him.

She solemnly walked to her room, packed her bag and headed toward the front door. She tiptoed to the nursery without a sound and opened the door. The glow of starry light shone on the wee babes like magical dust rising from their sweet angelic faces.

Smiling at their sweet wonder, she laid the embroidered pillow on the table next to the door, blew them a kiss and closed the door.

"Be well, my loves. Anam Cara," she whispered as she walked out the front door, down the elevator and out the main entrance of the Dakota for the last time into the street.

The chilled night breeze whipped around as she stood in front of the building, but inside she felt as frigid as the snow queen.

She looked in each direction, wondering which way to go. Then she saw the sun beckon a single light from the dark horizon and walked toward the light.

Chapter Twelve

Winter 1992

She walked around an hour in the cold darkness, not sure what to do and where to go. And as the morning sun peered up to its place, Maggie stopped and looked at the sun rise to begin a new day.

She felt a gleam of light warming the back of her head and turned around to find herself in front of the cathedral.

The warmth wrapped around her body and into her heart, summoning her into the church.

Setting her suitcase down, she walked up to the altar, lit a candle and knelt down in prayer.

"It's fairly early for prayer, my child," the priest said as he approached her.

"If I'm honest, Father, my faith is a bit shaken this day," she said.

"Ah, a soul of the Emerald Isle," he said and knelt next to her. "This is not the confessional, but you may unburden yourself. I am a good listener. It's a requirement." He looked at her with a warm and caring smile.

Maggie could hold it in no longer. With tears streaming down her face, she told the padre the entire saga of Bryne and Caroline, culminating in her homeless predicament.

"Damn me green-eyed Irish temper for betraying me and gettin' me in trouble. But I just couldn't help meself." She paused, catching her inappropriateness.

"Pardon me language, Father."

"I'd say you're justified. Well, if you're willing to travel a mite, I think I can help you. My sister lives in Chicago and her mistress is in need of help in her household. Do you have train fare?" the father asked.

Maggie nodded and paused in thought.

"A new city may be a blessing. I'd like to see more of this country at that," she said confidently.

"Then it is done." The father grabbed some paper, scribbled a note and handed it to Maggie.

"Here's my sister's address. Give this note to her as a form of introduction," he said.

"Thank ya and bless ya, Father. ... I didn't get your name," Maggie said, shaking his hand.

"Father Donnelly," he smiled.

Maggie smirked and her eyes lit up. This was a sign she made the right decision. Maybe they were kin, maybe they weren't, but the familiarity gave her hope for a new life in a new city.

Armed with directions from the father, she left the church and marched to the train station with new vigor and purpose.

Once settled on the train, she wrote her mother a letter.

Dearest Mother,

Ya warned me more than once about me temper and it has come to pass. The demon spawn forced himself on a poor young lass and put her in the family way. That was the last straw for me. I couldn't hold my ire and I gave it to him and good right in front of Carrie. The bastard lied to her, of course, and he pushed me down and whacked me one. With my Irish eyes, I'm sure it won't be my last. It was worth it, just to give him a piece of me mind.

I expect it from him who has no soul, but Carrie cut me to the quick. She looked at me as if I were the grim reaper himself.

The empty wounded look in her eyes will haunt me 'til the end of me days.

She may love him or she may be trapped in a life of her own making; I can't be certain. I pity the dark days for her, knowing the truth of the man. Her soul will weep.

Suzanne Rudd Hamilton

 But I guess there's no blame on her. What choice did she have? A woman in a new country with two small ones. What could she do?

 As I'm seeing through her eyes, I fear for my friend. He'll never be what she dreams and keep hurting her, he will. I'll pray for their souls.

 And now I am out on my sore keister. Don't mistake me, I'm glad to be out of that hell of a house. Blast to all of them.

 I'm afraid this has made me weary of men. I have a bad taste for the lot of them.

 Carrie, Molly and you. While I know you're glad for me, ya may have chosen a different path than birthing and raising a fatherless mongrel yourself.

 Seems the whole breed are put on this earth to their own pleasures at that.

 The past is just that. It's time for me to begin anew and turn another page.

 A kindly priest helped me and I'm traveling to Chicago for a new start. He's called Donnelly. They may be kin, but if not, I'm young and sturdy and I'm in America, the land of opportunity. I can make my own. I'll write again once I put down me roots.

 Your Maggie

On the long ride, Maggie marveled at everything that met her eyes as America glided by. She saw mountains that reached the sky, farm fields of wheat and corn, horses and cattle and long plains of nothing that stretched along the horizon for hours. They stopped at a few stations along the way, but instead of bustling cities, they seemed to be plopped in the middle of the vast wilderness, an oasis in a mirage.

As the conductor called the upcoming Chicago stop, she watched curiously as they passed one smokestack and square brick building after another plumed in blackened dust.

But when it cleared, she could see stately buildings in the distance. She remembered the same feeling as when she first crossed the harbor into New York. Scared at the unfamiliar and alien world, but excited for the new adventure.

The conductor advised her to take a streetcar to Prairie Avenue. When she walked out onto West Harrison Street from Grand Central Station, she saw the streets of Chicago bustling with activity—horses, carriages and people, similar to New York. But one thing she never laid eyes on was a new horseless streetcar. She heard they had them in New York, but not in the remote section of the Dakota.

The electric streetcar was sleek, like an open train car with no front and no end. Maggie chuckled a little at the strange and new innovation. She wondered how it went, but when she sat down and it began, she snickered, watching the people and the street underneath passing by effortlessly.

Stepping off the streetcar and walking down Prairie Avenue was intimidating. She heard someone on the streetcar call it "millionaires' row." Walking down the street gaping at one elaborate mansion after another, it was easy to believe the richest and most elite people in the city each tried to triumph their excess over the other.

Her head craned admiring the exquisitely big front curved bay windows in different colors and shapes of Victorian style. Some of the homes had rounded roofs and some squared, while others boasted pointed railings on the roof peaks, almost like jewelry adorning the sky.

She nearly tripped or ran into people several times, as she couldn't take her eyes off the fabulous manors.

Her new residence, Harmon House, was at the 2000 block of Prairie Avenue. It was more modest compared with the grandeur of the mansions she passed, but the smoothed edges of the white stone house with its circle peaks on the roof made her smile, as it reminded her of Windermere back in Ireland.

She went to the side of the home and knocked at the servants' door.

"I'm looking for Mrs. Donnelly," Maggie told the young uniformed man who answered the door.

He waved her in the door and pulled a chair out at the table for her. Maggie smiled, surprised at his nice manners for another servant.

She waited a few minutes, taking in the look of the servant dining area with the big table and rows of cabinets and cupboards on all sides. She glanced into the kitchen with its long preparation table with hanging pots overhead.

On one wall, she noticed a row of labeled bells, just like at Donegal Hall, to summon each individual service.

"I'm Mrs. Donnelly," said a red-haired middle-aged woman in a black dress with a lace collar. She had kind eyes and red freckled cheeks. Maggie stood up and immediately smiled—the woman bore a similar resemblance to her mother.

"I'm Maggie Donnelly. Father Donnelly gave me this note to give you," she said, handing her the note.

She quickly read the note and stared at Maggie.

"Do we know each other?" she asked.

"I was wondering the same thing. My people are in County Donegal," Maggie said.

"Sit down, lass, we may be kin. I believe I had some in County Donegal a long time ago. My people are a bit south in County Leitrim." She paused.

"So you're looking for work. What can you do?"

"I sew," Maggie said abruptly.

"Everyone sews. What have you done in a household?" she asked.

"Practically everything. I have been a house maid for Mrs. Stevens at Windermere, where I grew up and I was a lady's maid and housekeeper for her daughter, the Viscountess of Donegal. And I don't just sew. I make fashionable dresses and gowns," Maggie said with pride.

"Hmm. The missus may just like the idea of a personal seamstress. Well, Mrs. Harmon's lady's maid is leaving soon, but until then, all I can offer you is a maid position. It's a terrible reduction for you."

"I would be happy and grateful for any position," Maggie interrupted her.

"Ok, I'll show you to your room. You'll be bunking with me daughter, Fiona," she said and led her down the hall and up the stairs to her room, and then left her alone.

Maggie was thankful for the work and promised advancement but didn't see any uniform in the room and wasn't sure she had the proper attire for a maid. She went through her suitcase to see if she had her old maid uniform from Windermere.

She found the apron and mop cap but couldn't find a proper maid dress. She swiftly sifted through her black and dark green uniform dresses with white Irish lace collars and sleeves, the ones Katherine gave her when she left. But she could find no suitable maid's dress.

Taking out her sewing kit, she looked at a plain tan dress she had to go under her coat to see if she could alter it to work when a young blonde girl burst into the room rubbing her backside.

"You think he'd move the pinches around me bum, but he always gets me in the same place," she complained. "You're new. I'm Fiona."

"Hello. Who's pinching you?" Maggie asked, concerned she fell into another lion's den.

"Mr. Ambrose, the butler," she said in a matter-of-fact tone. "He's harmless, but he likes to pinch."

"Here, me ma thought you may not have a maid dress, so she asked me to give you this one."

Maggie held the dress up and saw its voluminous size.

"It was Bridget's. She liked to eat, but you can take it in," she said.

"You need to be quick, though; we need to start on the silver before dinner," she told Maggie.

With no time to alter, Maggie cut small holes in each side and tied ribbons through them to cinch it up. She put the apron and mop cap on and followed Fiona.

That night, Maggie stayed up late tailoring the dress to fit her and customized it a little with pockets. Uniformity was the key with maids, so she couldn't adorn it in any way.

She wondered if Fiona and Mrs. Donnelly were her kin. Given the uncanny resemblance to her mother, it was a possibility, but there was really no way to know. It comforted her just to know it was a chance.

At first light, Fiona and Maggie were hard at work cleaning the fireplace ash, dusting and polishing the furniture, cleaning the carpets and washing the windows, all before anyone rose for the day. Maids and the act of cleaning were never to be seen by the mister and missus.

When the Harmons and any guests woke and left for their breakfast, Maggie and Fiona changed the linens in the bedrooms, made the beds and cleaned the rooms and adjacent baths.

After the initial work of the day around eleven o'clock, they had their breakfast.

The first meal with the rest of the staff was enlightening for Maggie. There were more service staff than the Dakota apartment and Windermere, but far less than at Donegal Hall.

Maggie sat at breakfast eating, watching and listening. As this was her fourth household, she knew how important it was to understand the dynamics and relationships of each and every person.

John, the footman, was the very tall awkward young man with a high squeaky voice who first opened the door for Maggie. He was kind and obviously sweet on Fiona. He beamed with excitement every time she came into the room.

Mrs. Ambrose, the cook, was American and the wife of Mr. Ambrose, the butler. She was a small thin woman with gray hair and a permanently pursed look on her face. Her food was good, but she wasn't talkative and mostly kept to herself. Maggie wondered if she knew of her husband's antics with the staff.

Kate was her kitchen maid and aspiring assistant cook. In complete contrast to Mrs. Ambrose, she was tall, stocky and tough, but friendly with brown hair and eyes. Fiona said she grew up on a cattle ranch.

Mr. Conrad was the mister's valet. He had a serious, studious look about him and he was smart. Hehe read all the books of his former employer, who went to Harvard. He was always reading and loved to share tidbits of news and knowledge with everyone at meals.

Miss Thornton was the lady's maid. She was leaving soon to get married. All she could talk about was her upcoming nuptials and her new husband.

Then there was Mr. Ambrose. He introduced himself to Maggie just as Fiona warned. He looked her in the eyes with a devilish, creepy smile and shook her hand, holding it much too long. And when he sat down at the table, he pinched Maggie on the bottom as she went past.

The talk for the morning was minimal. Mr. Ambrose introduced Maggie and then went over the Harmons' activities for the day and any expectations.

"They just broke ground on the site for the World's Fair. It's called the Columbian Exposition commemorating the 400th anniversary of Columbus coming to America," Mr. Conrad read from the newspaper.

"And also the anniversary of me and Ma coming to America," Fiona laughed.

Suzanne Rudd Hamilton

"It also says 40,000 people will build it in Jackson Park," Mr. Conrad said.

"It will create a horrible mess. For the next two years, we'll be dodging people, dust and dirt," Mr. Ambrose scowled.

"Maggie, you sewed that dress so fine, you could never tell it was three times too big for you. You are a fine seamstress," Mrs. Donnelly remarked.

"You sew?" Miss Thornton asked, perking up.

Maggie nodded.

"I know this is a bit abrupt because we just met, but could you take a look at my wedding dress? I'm having some trouble with it and could use some advice."

"I'd be happy to after the day's work is done," Maggie smiled.

At the end of breakfast, Fiona and Maggie went into the laundry to clean the linens. Since they were alone, Fiona filled her in on everyone.

"Well, now you've met them. What do you want to know?" Fiona asked.

"Oh, I'm just glad to be here. I don't..." Maggie said and Fiona interrupted.

"Now then, no use in standing on ceremony. It's a peculiar bunch, they are," Fiona said.

"Well, I will say John seems to have a glimmer in his eyes for you. I'm wondering if ya do for him," she said.

"You're a quick minx, Maggie Donnelly," she laughed. "I know he's sweet on me. He's nice and I like the attention, but I'm not putting all me eggs in that basket before I see a little more of what's out there."

"And thanks for warning me about Mr. Ambrose," Maggie said.

"Poked ya already, did he?" Fiona said and Maggie nodded.

"I wonder if Mrs. Ambrose knows," Maggie said.

"It's your guess. That woman's locked up tighter than the church collection on Christmas Eve. She never says a word," Fiona said.

Chapter Thirteen

Maggie was exhausted. She was accustomed to hard work, but once word got out about her dressmaking skills, she found extracurricular duties helping Miss Thornton on her wedding dress and any number of corrections to Mrs. Harmon's wardrobe, plus advising others on this or that fix to their personal clothing or uniforms.

"I am so grateful for your help," Miss Thornton said. "My Earl will be so happy when he sees me in this dress. I can't wait to take care of just one man—my man—and his house for a change."

"It is different to be taking care of your own house," Maggie said.

"I want to repay you. Since you're taking my position, I'm going to tell you everything you need to know about Mrs. Harmon, so she'll like you right away," she offered.

Maggie knew the duties of a lady's maid, but as Caroline was her only mistress, she listened intently to Miss Thornton about Mrs. Harmon's needs, wants and eccentricities. A lady's maid needed to be indispensable to keep her employment.

Miss Thornton told Maggie that Mrs. Harmon was very interested in new fashion and precise about everything she wore and how she looked. She was far from being a deb, but she prided herself on wearing the latest trends and was known in society circles for her exquisite taste.

"She's lower on the totem pole in the ladies' group, as many more of them have bigger staffs and mansions and wealthier husbands, so she holds herself as the authority on fashion and is obsessed with looking the part," Miss Thornton explained.

Maggie appreciated the insight and decided to start the relationship with a bang. In her spare hours, she began making a detailed vest for Mrs. Harmon with a herringbone darted pattern. Maggie saw many ladies in New York wearing such an accessory over their garment, so she thought Mrs. Harmon would like it. Miss Thornton supplied the materials from the missus' leftover fabric.

She worked late into the night by gas lamp, bruising her fingers purple again, making her miss her Dakota sewing machine more and more.

During the day, she labored without a break, but found a few moments to write her mother.

Dearest Mother,

My new place is very nice and I'm getting settled. I forgot how much harder maid's work is, but it's honest.

Suzanne Rudd Hamilton

I'm promised a promotion to lady's maid again. I'm a little nervous. I hope the missus will like me. I'm making something for her to show my worth right away. As you always say, "Don't hide your light under a bushel or no one will see it."

The people here are nice. Mrs. Donnelly and Fiona may even be kin. Their people are from County Leitrim. They've treated me nice, but there are always strange ones.

Mr. Ambrose is the worst of them. Hand to God, the mister has grabbed hold of me backside more times a day than I count me holy cards. Some days I have to use liniment just so I can set down at night. Fiona says he's harmless, just a pincher, but I wonder if any men are harmless. They all seem to be out for themselves. I'll keep both my eyes on him, I will. Don't worry—I can take care of meself.

You taught me well. We didn't need any men in our lives, and I don't see as I'll need any either. I'm hoping to find a family here with the Donnellys. I don't know if they are relations, but I will believe it to be so. Will write soon.

Your Maggie

After the next morning's breakfast, Mrs. Donnelly asked Maggie to the butler's pantry where there was a strange man standing there in dirty workman's clothes.

"Maggie, this is the mason to fix the fireplace. Show him to the sitting room and mind his dirt. The mister and missus are out, so you won't be disturbed," Mrs. Donnelly said aloud to Maggie and pulled her aside and whispered in her ear.

"Watch him the whole time. You know about the Scottish—they steal."

Maggie motioned for her to follow him into the sitting room. She'd never met a Scottish person before, but the tales of the rivalries between the two sons of the British Empire were notorious.

Despite their many similarities and their equal hatred of the English, the people of Ireland and Scotland had a mistrust stemming from the fourteenth century War of the Three Kings that never healed.

Their shared language roots in Celtic and Gaelic, obedience to culture and to the Catholic Church and farming connections were always eclipsed by using each other as pawns in feuds with the English. Since they were on separate islands with water between, they never had a need to live in peace and harmony.

She watched him, curiously studying his features, as he worked repairing the fireplace bricks that were cracked and crumbling.

He was of average height, neither short nor tall and had curiously curly orangish-red hair under his cap. She heard many Scots had red hair, but this was unlike her darker auburn locks. She immediately noticed his muscular physique and firm, powerful arms. As a workman, he labored with his hands and arms all day, giving them rippling definition and alluring strength.

"Are yer watching me or trying to learn a trade?" He laughed and looked at her.

He was very dirty, so it was difficult to see his face, but she couldn't help but notice his striking blue eyes and nice crooked smile in the corner of his mouth.

"I'm just here while ya work. Go on with ya," Maggie said, embarrassed, and motioned for him to continue.

He chuckled and started working again. She was a little uncomfortable he caught her looking at him, but she didn't want to give him the satisfaction of admitting it. So she wiped down the furniture and patted down the upholstery close to the fireplace. Nothing was dirty, as she and Fiona cleaned a few hours earlier, but she wanted to look busy and she promised to keep an eye on him. She was interested in him, but also had to ensure nothing was taken.

"Are yer interested in the doings over at the fairground?" he asked.

"I've heard a little," she said nonchalantly, pretending to fluff the pillows.

"Well, if yer want to know anything, come to me. I'm working there, so yer can get it straight from the horse's mouth," he said while he continued working.

"I'll keep that in mind," she said in a matter-of-fact voice.

"It's going to be a marvel. Not much now, but I've talked to a bunch of the workers and pieced it all together. Lakes, bridges, buildings and wonders from all across the globe, all in one place. It's going to be better than anything ever seen before. And of course, the masonry will be the best in the world. Over 5,000 men, many Scots, will make sure of that," he boasted.

Maggie chuckled sarcastically.

"See, yer are wondering," he grinned.

"Good thing they have all your hot air to fire the bricks," she smiled.

"Now there yer go. I like a lass that gives as good as she gets," he laughed.

"I'm not here for ya to mind. Ya can just finish your work and be gone with ya," Maggie said feigning annoyance but was secretly intrigued.

"Nothing meant by that, I'll say. It's certainly my pleasure to find a pretty maid with rusted hair and fiery eyes to look at when I have to do me work," he said coyly.

Maggie smiled and unconsciously let out a brief giggle, then covered her mouth and lowered her head, not wanting to give away she was pleased by his words.

"I'll tell yer, the fair will take over 100,000 men to build her from the ground," he said casually.

"Ha! You're a forked-tongue phony, ya are," she countered, loudly pointing at him. "Mr. Conrad says a sum of 40,000 were hired. It says so in the newspaper. Ya probably don't even work there. Ya talk aside your arse."

She immediately realized what she said and lowered her head, ashamed she let her temper flare.

There was a brief moment of silence and then he laughed so hard, he fell on his bottom from his crouched perch with a loud thud.

"I like a redhead with a fierce temper," he said. "Reminds me of me mum."

"I'm terribly sorry." Maggie went over to him and offered him a hand. "I had no right to call ya a liar. At times I can't help meself."

Her hand touched his and she felt a tingle she never felt before shoot right up her arm; she pulled away quickly in surprise.

He smiled and got to his feet without saying a word and gathered his tools.

"My name is David McIntyre. Me mates call me Mac. Please to meet yer," he said and tipped his hat.

"I'm Maggie Donnelly," she said softly and escorted him to the door.

"I'd like to call on ya again, if that's all right," he said while standing in the doorway.

Maggie smiled and nodded, nearly breathless from the encounter, and closed the door behind him.

Chapter Fourteen

"A curse on me own mother for letting you watch the handsome workman instead of me," Fiona told Maggie as they were bedding for the night.

"It was nothing," Maggie said, secretly smiling.

"Nothing? I peeked in a few times and saw him. He's handsome. I wouldn't pass him up on the street. And go on with ya; I heard him flirting. I saw you pretending to polish the clean furniture," she said firmly.

"I had to watch him. Plus, I'm sure he's always like that. Men flirt with anyone they set eyes on," Maggie said, hoping to put the discussion to an end.

"Will he call again, I wonder?" Fiona said.

"It's out of me mind already and I'll bid ya goodnight," Maggie said.

That night, Maggie dreamed of the handsome Scot whisking her away to a farm of their own. Bringing her flowers every day and telling her how much he loved her, surrounded by their house full of children.

Asleep, her dreams seemed possible, but in the stark reality of the workday and the first pinch of the morning from Mr. Ambrose, she realized they were just dreams; reality was quite different.

"Here's an article about the fair construction," Mr. Conrad said. "They hired a man named Olmstead to create the lakes, bridges and rivers. This says he designed Niagara Falls center and Central Park in New York."

Maggie's ears perked up. The Scot was right. He talked about lakes and bridges at the fair. Maybe he was telling the truth.

She remembered her wonderful walks with the pram through Central Park and imagined how wonderful it would be to see something like that again in Chicago.

After breakfast, everyone went back to work and Mrs. Donnelly called Maggie to her room.

"Miss Thornton leaves at the end of the week and I'll have a new girl starting then to work with Fiona. You will begin as the mistress's lady's maid on Saturday. The missus will be out until Sunday, so you can get adjusted and take the rest of the time off," Mrs. Donnelly informed her and sat down at her desk.

Maggie nodded and paused for a minute.

"Is there something else?" Mrs. Donnelly asked.

"Yes, I wanted to know what ya thought of men," Maggie said.

Mrs. Donnelly put down her pen and briefly stared at Maggie before answering.

"Well, in my experience, some are good, some are bad and most of the lot are in between. Is this about Mr. Ambrose?" she asked.

Embarrassed by her question, Maggie quickly shook her head no and abruptly left the room.

Working in the laundry that day, she listened in silence while Fiona went on and on about men. She talked about what she liked in men. What her ideal man would look like, what he would say, and on and on.

Deep in thought, Maggie daydreamed deep in thought about men, too, but focused on their character. Pretty eyes and bulging muscles were fine to look at, but they didn't do Caroline or her own mother any good.

Growing up without a father, Maggie's entire worldview of men was from watching how lecherous men like Bryne and Mr. Ambrose took advantage of women for their own pleasures.

At a young age, Katherine was honest with her daughter about her absent father as a cautionary tale.

"He was a young stable hand who came to Windermere to train a horse Mr. Stevens bought for Caroline's birth," Maggie remembered.

With rugged tanned skin and hazel eyes, Katherine was wooed by his good looks and flowery words promising sunshine, rainbows and everlasting love. He told Katherine when he earned enough money, they would get a farm and raise a family together.

Katherine said when she looked into his eyes, they were so clear and earnest, she believed his beautiful words and intentions were true. And because she wanted him and that life so much, she gave him certain privileges.

Then he moved on to his next job and never wrote her back. When she found herself in the family way with Maggie, Mrs. Stevens took pity on her and allowed her to remain at Windermere. For a poor unwed girl with a bastard child, life could have been tragic for both of them.

The pain and hurt in her mother's eyes when she spoke of him burned into Maggie's memory and developed her mistrust of men. Then Bryne and Mr. Ambrose's selfish behavior painted a constant canvas in her mind of what men were like.

She didn't want to fall into that same love well that trapped Caroline and left her mother alone.

"Maggie, are you all right? John's talking to you," Fiona said, interrupting her deep thoughts.

"This came to the door for you just now," John said and handed her a note and a daisy.

It was from David McIntyre:

I'll be at The Times pub on Saturday night, if you can join me for a pint. I hope you do.

"Don't leave me wondering," Fiona said. "What does it say?"

Maggie hesitated. She wasn't sure she wanted to tell Fiona or give away her interest, but she immediately decided it may be good to bring a friend to avoid a romantic entanglement.

"He invited me to the pub for a pint Saturday night. Would ya like to come?" Maggie asked.

"Would I like to? If there's men like him, of course, you ninny," Fiona laughed.

Maggie sniffed the flower's clean fragrance and smiled, partially looking forward to seeing him but unsure of the path it may lead her on.

Before Miss Thornton left, she wanted to formally introduce Maggie to Mrs. Harmon. Even though Maggie worked as a chambermaid for several months, she never had any contact with the Harmons.

Maggie heard many things about missus Harmon from Fiona and Miss Thornton about her high standards and detailed and unrelenting attention to her wardrobe, so she was anxious to meet her and excited to give the missus the vest she made for her.

"Missus, this is Maggie Donnelly; she'll be taking over as lady's maid starting Saturday. She's a wonderful seamstress and has an eye for the newest styles. She did wonders with my mother's old wedding dress," Miss Thornton said.

Mrs. Harmon was a tall stunning woman in her late 40s. She had chestnut brown hair and tanned skin, as she had a famous penchant for outdoor sports like tennis.

Irish Eyes

"I thought ya may like this vest, ma'am," Maggie said, handing her the garment. "This style is very popular in New York."

Mrs. Harmon's brown eyes lit up when she saw the detail of the herringbone design.

"This is fabulous, Donnelly. Oh, no, that will be too confusing with Mrs. Donnelly. Hmm. We will need to call you something else. What was your mother's name?" Mrs. Harmon asked.

"Donnelly, ma'am." Maggie said softly and looked down, afraid of what Mrs. Harmon would think.

"Oh, well then, we need a name for you. Where are you from?" she asked.

"County Donegal in Ireland, Mrs. Harmon" Maggie said.

"Excellent; I will call you Donegal," Mrs. Harmon said, admiring the workmanship of the vest. "If you can make more things like this, you will indeed be my new secret weapon, Donegal."

Maggie forced a smile and left the room, seething at the idea of being called Donegal every day, a horrid reminder of the cause of her breakup with Caroline. But a lady's maid cannot be called by a first name, like a chambermaid. And there would be confusion with the same surname as the housekeeper. She would just have to live with it. Only a few years in America and part of her name would be lost again.

Suzanne Rudd Hamilton

Since Mrs. Harmon left for the weekend, the next day, Saturday, Maggie looked around Mrs. Harmon's room to familiarize herself with her wardrobe. Maggie spent a few hours organizing the dresses, clothing and jewelry to her more efficient style, making it easier for her to coordinate the outfits for a complete look.

She also took an accounting of all the dresses and wardrobe pieces and made notes to discuss suggestions for improvements with Mrs. Harmon.

With the rest of the day to herself, she focused on her own wardrobe for her evening outing.

Since she had arrived in Chicago, she had worn only her uniform and rarely left the house. The only remaining pieces she had were her traveling suit, a plain tan work dress, a farm dress she brought from Ireland and her church dress.

Since her church dress and traveling suit were too formal for a pub, she decided to improve the farm dress for the evening. The cotton dress was an appealing cornflower blue with small white flowers, but it was plain. For her first evening out in America—with a man—Maggie wanted to look sophisticated.

Taking some fabric pieces from her saved stock, she fashioned two stiff white cuffs and a collar for the dress, then made tied a bow from some yellow fabric. She didn't have enough time or fabric to make a vest like Mrs. Harmon's, so she concocted a waistband vest from tan fabric with two buttons and made armholes, like suspenders for over her shoulders, to cinch her waist and show off her bustline.

Maggie let her hair down some and placed her straw hat on her head when Fiona came in.

"That's grand. With you looking like a fancy picture postcard, I'm going to look like a banshee in this old dress," Fiona remarked.

Maggie took a few ribbons and hastily spiced up Fiona's dress.

"You're a miracle worker, that you are!" Fiona beamed, twirling in joy at the updated look of her old dress.

The two walked arm in arm a few blocks to The Times pub. They asked John for directions, since young men often frequented pubs in their off hours. When they told him where they were going, John offered to accompany them, but Fiona made a face and he said Mr. Ambrose probably wouldn't let him leave anyway. He told them that the pub was near the factories, so it was a popular destination for men and women from the sweatshops to spend their few hours of leisure.

Maggie and Fiona didn't know what to expect, as neither had ever visited a pub before. They found the women's entrance at the side of the pub. John told them about that and walked in hand in hand.

The pub was very loud and smelled of sour beer and they found the sawdust on the floor under their feet strange. But they were immediately absorbed in the infectious merriment of the men and women they saw, laughing and singing along with a tinny-sounding piano, while hoisting their glasses. It put them at ease.

Maggie scanned the room until she saw David McIntyre. He was standing at the bar with a pipe sticking out of his mouth and drinking a pint with several other men, at the same time.

He was clean and dressed in a nice plaid shirt and tan pants with a vest and kerchief tied in a knot around his neck. His cap was off, so she could see the volume of his fire-colored curly hair sitting atop his head.

When he saw her, he waved her over to him, grinning with his coy smile. She was impressed by how nice he looked without the workday dirt she saw before. She could even see the slight pink hue in his skin and cute freckles on his nose. And the pipe gave him an alluring regal quality.

"Well, he cleaned up nice," Fiona teased.

They walked over to the bar, where he introduced the girls to his friends and gave them each pints of beer.

"I'm happy to see yer," he said as he handed her the pint.

The group was a cordial and jolly bunch. Several girlfriends and wives of the men joined in, which made Maggie and Fiona feel more comfortable. While in village pubs in Ireland, it was common for country women to drink with the men. John told them in America only women accompanied by a man would imbibe in mixed company.

"This is me home away from home," Mac explained. It's run by an Irishman, but he's ok. It reminds me of a village pub back home. He added some Scottish and English bits with the Irish stuff to make us all feel at home. Back home, you'd never see this lot together. A few pints and some good whiskey make us all brothers in America."

As this was an Irish pub and mostly Irish, English and Scottish patrons, they welcomed women.

Fiona was happily flirting with the men, while they taught her to play pub games like Dart and Target and Aunt Sally.

She giggled as the attentive men showed her how to throw the darts at the target and sticks at "Aunt Sally," a round cloth ball with a pipe sticking from her mouth.

Maggie smiled as she watched Fiona laugh and flirt. When Mac tried to teach her how to throw sticks, she pursed her lips and took the sticks from him, knocking the pipe out in only a few throws.

He grinned and scrunched his eyebrows in pleasant disbelief at her aim.

Maggie laughed at his reaction.

"Don't be surprised. I grew up on a farm; we used to knock everything off a rail with a gallybander just for something to do."

He took Maggie to a nearby booth where they could watch their friends but could talk privately.

She marveled at his charming demeanor. It seemed as though he knew everyone in the pub, as people said "Hello Mac" and "Nice to see you" as they passed him.

"You're a popular fella, Mac," she said.

"Nah, just fellas I work with," he laughed. "They never see me with a girl, so they're making eyes at you."

"That's a fine tale you'll tell," Maggie remarked with a sarcastic smile.

"Yer don't believe me?" he asked. "No other lass could catch my eye with yer around?"

Maggie didn't believe he was shy or often without female companionship, but as she gazed into his striking blue eyes, she was arrested to distraction by their allure. All she could do was smile.

As the evening wore down, he insisted on accompanying them back to Harmon House to ensure their safety. Trying to avoid a romantic goodnight scene, Maggie initially resisted, but then reluctantly agreed—it was late and she was unsure of the streets at that hour.

Outside the smoky pub, she was captivated by the rich fragrance of his pipe smoke in the dark night. He regaled them as they walked the few blocks with talk of the amazing sights developing at the fairgrounds.

When they reached the side entrance of Harmon House, Fiona started to go in and Maggie secretly grabbed her hand to keep her in place.

"Thank ya for a wonderful evening," Maggie said.

"I hope to see yer again." He smiled, tipped his cap, and strode away into the dark night.

When they were safely in the door and up to their room, Maggie grinned, inhaling the smell of his pipe smoke on her dress.

"I haven't had that much fun in me whole life," Fiona said. "Please say we can do that again.

Still grinning, Maggie sighed and nodded, then turned out the light, ready to dream wonderful thoughts.

Chapter Fifteen

The next morning, Maggie helped Fiona get wood for the fireplace boxes, clean out the ash and dust the furniture.

As it was Sunday, she, Fiona and Mrs. Donnelly changed into their church dresses, grabbed some quick bread for breakfast and went to Mass at St. James Catholic Parish a few blocks away.

Mrs. Harmon was a staunch churchgoer allowed her household staff time for church every Sunday, as she and Mr. Harmon were out of the house attending services at their Presbyterian church. She permitted the staff to make up the hour off for church in the evening.

Maggie updated her lady's maid dress with the stiffer cuffs and collar she made for her day dress and reused the Irish lace from her mother on her Sunday morning dress.

As she donned her lady's maid dress for the first time in months, she picked up the cameo brooch Caroline gave her and debated wearing it.

"It is a nice cameo and my one piece of jewelry, so who cares where I got it? I earned it," Maggie said to herself and pinned the cameo to her new stiff collar.

Dearest Mother,

I hope you're getting on well. You mentioned some gout in your last letter. I know you love your sweets, but please take care to stay well. Mrs. Stevens can't get along without you for even a day.

I'm starting to work for Mrs. Harmon now. She's nice enough, but full of her looks and her place, she is. Me being a seamstress put stars in her eyes and now she has me making all manner of changes to her wardrobe, with new pieces and updates. She loves the stiff collars and cuffs I made for me dress, so now I'm outfitting all her daily wear with them.

And her status rose the minute she walked out the door and told all her hens that she has a personal dressmaker on her staff. And she puffs out her chest with pride when she tells them I used to be the private dressmaker for a viscountess. She skips the part about me being her lady's maid, though.

She bought a new shiny sewing machine for me, so I can quickly make her new clothes and updates. The hand sewing was taking too long for her taste. My fingertips thank her. Just like you say, it doesn't matter where the cow gets the milk, as long as you get to drink it.

Suzanne Rudd Hamilton

And I have me own room again, which gives me more space for my sewing. There's a ball coming up for the missus, so I have the most beautiful fabrics spread everywhere. I mind what you taught me and save every scrap I can. I'm making a new going out dress for meself. See, I met a man. A Scot. His name is David McIntyre.

We've only gone out for an hour or two here and there, as our times off are not the same. We meet with friends, but I don't mind telling ya that I think I'm starting to have more than just friend feelings for him.

I'm still not sure. He's a grand man. Handsome and strong and kind, he is. I can see it in the eyes. And sure he is with the funny words. I give it to him and he sends in back and good. I like him.

He's a Scot after all, but worse, he's a man. I don't know if I want that for meself. Even though I'm a maid and have little freedom now, I have plans. I think I could become a proper seamstress or dressmaker and be me own woman. Wouldn't that be something? Daughter of a housekeeper becomes a dressmaker? In me dreams it's real. If I start having babies and scrubbing down a house, that is what I'll be and with less to myself than I have now.

I know it's not in the Good Book to be selfish and not bring new life into this world, but does every woman have to do it? Mrs. Harmon doesn't have any children and she's God-fearing.

For now, I'll be settled with the nice company when I can get it.

Your darling Maggie

As the months went by, the whole city was abuzz with talk of the Columbian Exposition World's Fair. Everyone rarely spoke of anything else.

Mr. Conrad read news pieces daily about what the fair would include.

"This says there will be more than 65,000 items and exhibitions of new inventions created," he said.

"I heard there will be exotic people from the Far East showing native dances and hoochie coochie shows," Fiona laughed.

"Well, I don't know what that is, but this entry indicates that all states and forty-six different countries around the world will exhibit, including most of the European countries. Even uncivilized lands from the farthest parts of the globe will send native people to the fair," Mr. Conrad stated.

"What a treat. It'll be like taking a trip all around the world in just one day," Kate said excitedly.

"I'm not in favor of importing so many native people to our streets. What if they get out?" Mrs. Ambrose said with a sneer.

"I'm sure they'll keep them locked up with all the other foreigners who come to your shores, Mrs. America," Mrs. Donnelly said sarcastically.

Mrs. Harmon was on the ladies' committee to help the Board of Lady Managers with the Woman's Building exhibit. Since the most powerful women in the city were helpful with lobbying for the selection of Chicago as the fair's site, they persuaded the House of Representatives to amend the site designation bill to ensure a women's commission advised on the fair. They would also oversee the Woman's Building exhibit that would be designed by women and display only works of art, literature, music, and advances by women in the fields of science and home economics.

Daily, Mrs. Harmon told Maggie of all the ins and outs of gossip, arguments and progress of the society ladies planning this big endeavor.

"Donegal, I need a nice but easily cleanable dress, like a work dress, for today. We're going to the site to see our building," she told Maggie. "It's simply going to be stunning. Mr. Burnham is calling it the White City, since all the structures will be dressed in solid white stucco to be gleaming clean and bright. And our architect, a woman, has designed some gold accents. It will be gorgeous inside and outside. There will be murals, art and sculptures with a spectacular interior design, all done by women. It will be the best of the entire fair."

And Maggie got the inside chatter from Mac about the construction. Every time they met, he amused her with tales of the marvelous sites sprouting up right before his eyes.

Maggie smiled and gazed at him as he regaled the pub goers as he spun the yarn of the beautiful buildings and amazing sights going up at the fairgrounds. Maggie was entranced by his storytelling prowess. He spoke with such enthusiasm and precision, detailing everything he viewed; she almost felt like she was seeing it too.

Sometimes at night, if the Harmons were out, she could steal away and they walked down by the fairgrounds.

"Here's where they will set a great golden lady inside the big reflecting pond in the middle of the buildings. It is supposed to be like the lady in the New York Harbor I saw when I came over," he said, pointing it out to her.

"I saw her too when I landed. But I really want to see the Central Park land architect's work. I admired it so when I strolled Moira and Liam's prams through the park in New York. The rolling green grass reminded me of home and gave me a place to let off steam when I was ready to push the mister from the window to his death," she said.

"Well, I promise never to make yer that mad," he said. She smiled and tapped him on the arm for making fun of her.

"There won't be much grass here, though. They've accounted for every square foot to be covered with something. And they have this fool idea of coating all the buildings in the Court of Honor white. That's where all the big exhibits will be. We lads all scratched our heads when we heard that. Whoever heard of a bunch of white stucco buildings? I don't know how they'll keep them that way," he chuckled.

"If Mrs. Harmon and the ladies have anything to say about it, those buildings best stay white. She keeps talking about how stunning everything will be. It's very exciting," Maggie said.

She enjoyed their strolls very much. For a few months, they walked over to the site once a week, when either the Harmons went out for the evening to the theatre or a dinner party. It was difficult to pair their working schedules, since fair workers began early in the morning and didn't finish until darkness, and so did she, with only Sunday morning and Thursday afternoon off.

He brought her different flower stems for her coat lapel and hat every time he came to the door. She suspected he nicked them from gardens of the mansions on Prairie Avenue, since wildflowers were few and far between in a big city and florist flowers were expensive. But the thought was sweet and considerate.

Under the light of the moon, he would take her to specific areas outside the site gates, where they could see the buildings rise and the grounds take shape. With a gleam in his eyes, he would narrate the construction with so much energy, as if he were the architect.

They didn't have a chaperone, but they strolled for only an hour or so, giving them a chance to get to know each other. Maggie looked forward to their time together with anticipation not only for the insight to the fair but she also enjoyed spending time with him. They told each other about their families, their homelands and work. He kept up with her quick-witted tongue with gibes of his own and made her laugh.

As he walked her home one night, he lightly took her hand as she started for the door.

"I wanted to know. Well, I'm asking yer to come to the fair with me when it opens," he said looking deeply into her eyes. "It would be my honor to escort my best girl."

Startled, Maggie blurted a quick excuse.

"They say ya need to spend at least a day there or nothing. I don't usually have that much time," she said.

"Please ask if yer can get a Sunday off. I don't work on Sundays," he said with a smile. He gently squeezed her hand. "It will be months until the public can go, but I'll need that time to save up. I want to show my girl the best of the fair in style, like yer deserve."

Maggie smiled and bid him a hasty goodbye, then walked in the door.

"His girl—his best girl. He said it twice," she said, huffing in a little panic.

"Whose best girl?" Mr. Ambrose asked coming out of the shadows, startling her for the second time in only a few minutes.

"No one, Mr. Ambrose," she said, annoyed at his interruption, and walked past him.

"I'll let yer be my girl," he said. He grabbed the back of her skirt and placed his hand firmly on her bottom.

She usually quietly ignored his advances, but as she was already agitated, she pushed his hand away and fiercely objected. "I'll be thanking ya to let me go. I'm no one's girl," she said sternly with her eyes flared. She stomped off up to her room.

As she took off her coat and hat, she breathed heavily in anger at Mr. Ambrose's lechery and at Mac's impertinence. She sat on her bed frightened and seething at the idea of being possessed by anyone.

Even though Mac had been a perfect gentleman with her at all times, unlike the other men she knew, she was angry at his assumption that she was his girl. Especially when she didn't know if that's what she wanted.

Mrs. Harmon already promised to give the household staff one whole day off to visit the fair, so she knew she could go, but when he called her his girl, it conjured a life and relationship that rattled her to the very core.

As it was time for Mrs. Harmon to return from a party, she composed herself and walked to the foyer to await her arrival.

Mrs. Harmon stomped into the foyer grumbling and seething with anger.

"I just can't believe that man. That insolent man!" Mrs. Harmon raged and waved to Maggie to follow her to her room.

Maggie had never seen Mrs. Harmon that upset. She was agitated and murmuring while Maggie took off her dress, then plopped in her chair in a blustering for Maggie to take down her hair.

"Some people are the most pompous, bombastic individuals on the planet," she fumed. "Calling us the Wild West and crude society. How dare he!"

Mrs. Harmon explained that Mrs. Cutler's cousin, a New York society matron wrote to her asking about the accommodations and entertainment the Chicago society would put on for the New York matrons when they came to visit the fair.

She wrote back that the society ladies in Chicago planned to host several balls, theatres and parties, a complete agenda to showcase Chicago culture to the New Yorkers. Mrs. Harmon said they wanted to make them feel welcome and rub their coup de gras of landing the fair in their noses.

But Mrs. Cutler's cousin sent her a newspaper column written by the self-proclaimed king of New York society and arbiter of all good taste, Mr. Ward McAllister, which warned his New York matrons to lower their expectations for a trip to Chicago.

"He thinks we don't know how to properly chill wine and our native food is rough and not up to the standards of their Eastern palates. And he quipped that we have no French chefs and would have to import them for their visit. But they're pleased that their sophisticated boys may find some hearty Middle West girls to marry here. The very nerve!" Mrs. Harmon ranted in a whirlwind of anger.

Maggie listened to her with interest, nodding in agreement and rallying in solidarity about men and their assumptions. But then she suddenly realized that Caroline and Bryne might come from New York to stay for the fair. Before then, she never contemplated seeing them again.

Her concern grew as Mrs. Harmon rattled off all the people who would stay with their wealthy Chicago counterparts or rent homes in the area.

She didn't hear Caroline's name, so she hoped maybe they weren't coming, but thought it was likely they would attend.

"And do you know what we're going to do? We're going to have the Chicago newspapers print editorials about Mr. McAllister in newsprint and send them to all of New York society," she said confidently. "We came up with a few zingers. The best one was, *Good heavens, Mr. McAllister, did you get the impression that the World's Fair is to be held for the benefit of New York society*?"

She cackled an evil laugh that unnerved Maggie a bit.

"He will rue the day he waged war with the Chicago elite," she proclaimed.

With that resolved, Maggie left her for the night and went back to her room.

Now she had two things to worry about. She worried about seeing Caroline again but decided that unless they came through the door of Harmon House, it was unlikely their paths would meet.

But she needed to figure out what to do about Mac. She would love to go with him and their gang to see the fair, but she didn't think it would be as a couple.

And there was that "best girl" comment. In her blissful friendship with Mac, she didn't realize he felt they were leading that way. She didn't know if she wanted to marry anyone or be part of a couple. But she did like him. She really liked him.

As the morning came early, she decided to sleep on the matter and hoped an answer would come.

In the morning, when the solution still eluded her, she asked Mrs. Donnelly for advice. Whether they were of the same family or not, Maggie came to know Mrs. Donnelly and Fiona as family in Chicago. Ever since she arrived, Mrs. Donnelly treated her the same as Fiona, good or bad, like her own.

"Mrs. Donnelly, would it be wrong if I never wanted to marry or have children?" Maggie asked.

"Well, the Good Book says the way to honor the Lord Almighty is to bear and care for children. And me mother always said it's easy to halve the potato where there's love. But she also said, you've got to do your own growing, no matter how tall your father was. So, if you don't mind me saying so, this is a new world here in

America. Your book hasn't been written. You write it according to you," she said.

Maggie smiled and squeezed her hand, thanking her for her wise words. Mrs. Donnelly's way of spinning old wives' wisdom into a conversation reminded Maggie of her mother so much, it made her miss home and her mother less.

She could carve her own path, but the question was whether she liked Mac enough to want him to plow one alongside her.

The next time Mac took her on a walk, she knew she had to answer his question. After all, he just asked to take her to the fair, not for her hand.

"I wanted to let ya know I'll be pleased to go to the fair with ya, but I insist to pay for the entry ticket and one ride. Ya can do the rest," she said.

He smiled with a crooked grin and shook her hand in agreement. She was glad that was out of the way and they could focus on the excitement leading up to the fair.

Throughout the fair's two-year construction, changes and finances delayed the project to create a mad rush for the dedication of the fair on October 21, 1892, a couple weeks late of the 400th anniversary of Columbus' landing.

The official opening of the exhibits and attractions would officially open on May 1, 1893.

But in the few weeks before the dedication, Mac could steal only moments here and there as the fair workers toiled around the clock to get it completed on time for the preopening.

Even when he couldn't meet her, every week he would leave flowers and a note at the door.

One morning, when he went outside to pick up wood for the fireplaces, John picked up the note and flowers and gave it to Maggie. It read:

Since I couldn't peek me head in to see your beautiful face and green eyes, I wanted yer to have these pretty posies to brighten your day. Mac

"Fancy having a man give me flowers and love notes all the time," Fiona joked.

"He's a very nice friend." Maggie smiled and inhaled the fragrant flowers.

"He's sweet on you and if you're not on him, my arse isn't sore from Mr. Ambrose's pinches," she scolded. "You and your Irish stubbornness just won't see it."

"Well then, lucky you. Mine is plenty sore," Maggie answered smartly.

"Is he taking ya to the fair?" she asked.

"Yes," Maggie said.

"John, Kate, and I will go, unless I get a better offer," she said.

Chapter Sixteen

The Columbian Exposition World's Fair was the most exciting event in memory to happen in Chicago. The buildup was on everyone's lips.

Maggie was busy making a new dress for Mrs. Harmon to attend the exclusive dedication of the fair. It was going to be the event of the century for Chicago's elite, and Mrs. Harmon was right in the center of the hoopla.

"Donegal, this dedication is going to be incredible. First, there will be a parade. People say it will be the largest parade ever held in Chicago and have more dignitaries than found in Washington, DC. I heard 75,000 people will participate. And on the day of the dedication, there will be a carriage parade of the most important people leading into the fair gates with no less than President Harrison at the lead." Mrs. Harmon was giddy with anticipation.

She allowed the staff to view the parade for one hour, as long as they made up the hour at the end of the day.

Maggie, Fiona, Kate, John, Mr. Conrad, and Mrs. Donnelly all dressed in their Sunday best to stand amid the other million people who attended to view the spectacle.

The others had seen parades before, including on the 4th of July or other occasions, but agreed this one was special.

Maggie was in awe of the people and the pageantry, as this was her first parade in America. Her eyes and head quickly darted back and forth to see everything in her view.

Celebratory banners, buntings, streamers and flags of the stars and stripes were draped all over the buildings.

"It looks like the 4th of July in October," Mr. Conrad said, happily waving a red, white and blue flag.

Maggie enthusiastically waved at the processional rows of Sousa's Chicago brass band, a Mexican national band and military guard of the Grand Army of the Republic and local academy cadets on Michigan Boulevard began the parade to Jackson Park, followed by carriages and horses with governors, mayors, senators and other politicians and dignitaries.

She was thrilled to see an endless array of thousands of men march with civic groups, including the Independent Order of Foresters, Patriotic Order of Sons of America, Consolidated Temperance Societies and Veterans and Sons of Veterans, all in full regalia and uniform.

And when assemblages from Ireland and Scotland strode in line with other foreign national societies from

Suzanne Rudd Hamilton

Croatia, Germany, Poland, Sweden and Scandinavia, she thought her heart would burst open with pride.

Fiona, Maggie, and Mrs. Donnelly gave an extra loud cheer when the sons of Ireland walked in front of them.

The parade seemed endless with new collections of people at every turn. Maggie started to wonder if there was anyone left to watch the parade as all souls in the city seemed to be joining.

"Every able man in the city is marching before us. There's no one left in any building or pub right now," Mrs. Donnelly laughed.

She even saw mounted police and officers on foot lining the route to accompany all the groups in the parade. A float commemorating Columbus' journey in 1492 was accompanied by 8,000 Italian men in drawn by 10 horses.

"I've never seen such a thing in me whole life," Maggie marveled with a big smile and eyes as big as saucers, like a kid on Christmas Day.

The next day for the dedication, the workers were given a day off, so Mac and Maggie went strolling to look at the scene.

"Surin they know how to put on a celebration here in America," Maggie laughed at the grandeur.

"This is just a bunch of glad-hand politicians showing off. The real show will be the fair itself. There's nothing like it on Earth," Mac said.

"I'm can hardly wait eight months to see all your hard work," Maggie smiled.

In April, Maggie was again hard at work on a new suit for Mrs. Harmon to attend the opening day of the fair. Mrs. Harmon purchased a lady's version of a dandy top hat with feathers and ribbons and wanted a herringbone suit to match the vest Maggie made for her the year before.

The intricate detail of the suit was easier in the lighter linen fabric, but it took every hour of Maggie's time to complete it.

Mac was working round the clock with the laborers in a fever pitch again in the cold and rainy spring days to finish the fair construction. Right until the minute people walked through the gates, paintbrushes were applying white to the Court of Honor buildings and others were putting in landscaping and other final touches. Even then, the jewel of the fair, the engineering marvel of the Ferris wheel, lay in its skeletal state, unfinished until a month later.

After the opening ceremonies, Mrs. Harmon was so excited she gathered the staff in the sitting room to regale them with the events of the day.

"It was simply fabulous. We rode up in the carriage and stood next to the podium. All the ladies who participated in the committees, like myself, were allowed at the front. There were speeches by our new president, Grover Cleveland; the Duke of Veragua, a direct descendent of Christopher Columbus; and the archbishop of Ireland. Our Woman's Building was the showcase of the fair. And Miss Susan B. Anthony stood in the Gallery of Honor and spoke about advancement of women throughout history next to the Modern Woman exhibit.

"And then the president pressed a golden telegraph key to start the electric lights that surrounded the fair. They sparkled like diamonds and Christmas tree candles. It was the most amazing thing I'd ever seen in my life," she said with sheer enthusiasm.

Maggie and the rest of the staff walked out of the room with smiles on their faces and visions dancing in their heads, awaiting their chance to see the magnificent fair with their own eyes.

"This article says there were over 200,000 people at the fair on opening day to see the six hundred acres of fairgrounds with 200 buildings and hundreds of statues and fountains. It says the Columbia Exposition is the largest world's fair ever held," Mr. Conrad read from the morning paper the day after the opening.

Maggie listened with interest and wonder that she was lucky enough to lay her Irish eyes on the largest fair in history.

Since the New York elite delegation was visiting in May, the staff's turn would need to wait, as they were busy hosting parties as well as visitors for tea, lunch and dinner.

Maggie didn't know if Bryne and Caroline visited Chicago with their society friends, but they didn't walk through the Harmon House door and Mrs. Harmon did not speak of them.

The fireworks that began with Mr. Ward McAllister and the New York society ladies seemed to simmer during their monthlong visit. Mrs. Harmon didn't mention any strife, but instead gabbed about all the people she met and their wonderful clothes, giving Maggie notes for wardrobe changes and additions here and there.

With leftover scraps from Mrs. Harmon, she made some changes to her traveling suit skirt, adding a full herringbone vest and using her Irish lace to make gloves. And she made a few touches for Fiona, Kate and Mrs. Donnelly.

On a bright sunny Sunday in June, it was finally her time. It was fair day.

She dressed Mrs. Harmon for the day early, changed quickly and eagerly waited outside the door for Mac.

He approached, smiling and donning his Sunday best; he carried a small bouquet of lovely flowers.

"These posies are not nearly as beautiful as yer are, but I figured yer could wear them in your hat and show off that red hair," he said and arranged the stems in her straw hat.

"That was very sweet. I'm so excited, I can barely stand myself," Maggie said, taking his arm for their stroll to the fairgrounds.

From her first through the gates, Maggie's eyes widened in wonder. The newspaper accounts and word-of-mouth tales of the grand White City paled in comparison with her green eyes looking at the real thing.

It was magnificent—the most brilliant collection of crisp and clean white buildings she could imagine.

The expansive, elegant neoclassical Court of Honor buildings created a U-shaped mirror of glistening reflection in the water basin in the center. Behind the sparkling fountain stood a series of Roman columns topped with alabaster statues overlooking the lakefront, as if standing guard. A giant glittering gold Grecian lady towered over the spectacle like a golden key welcoming entry.

Mac smiled with pride looking at the astonishment on her face.

"Pretty good for a former swamp," he said.

Among the sea of black bowlers and straw hats, Maggie and Mac moved in a daze gaping in awe at the magical city created in less than two years.

"What do yer want to do first, me lassie?" Mac asked, taking her hand. "I've a pocket full of nickels and the world is your oyster."

Maggie knew he saved for months to spare the cost of several days' wages to give her this once-in-a-lifetime experience. Per their agreement, he let her pay the fifty cents for each ticket. Since she was worried he didn't have a lot saved, she showed the most interest in the free exhibitions to see as much as they could and save their pennies for a special ride or two.

For hours, they viewed the art and beautiful pieces of grand china, glass, and glamorous textiles from all over the world. They walked through many pavilions displaying the latest innovations in machinery and invention that were expected to usher in a new century of prosperity.

One of the most memorable was the hulking Edison tower of lights that was choreographed in time to the *Blue Danube* waltz.

Touring "Little Europe" to sample the architecture, music, food and drink from abroad, Maggie felt a comforting warmth she hadn't experienced since she left the Emerald Isle.

"Try this beer," she boasted. "There's nothing in the world like an Irish stout."

"Maybe, but it doesn't top a Scotch whiskey and a bagpipe ceòl mòr," he joked.

"If ya don't mind me saying, it sounds like when the cow gave birth," Maggie laughed.

Then they passed a sign that read "Guinness Irish 1893 blue ribbon winner as World's Fair best beer."

Maggie laughed and poked Mac's arm as he lowered his head in defeat.

And so started the playful but proud banter arguing which display was better, Ireland's or Scotland's. The tiebreaker was the Gallery of Beauty visit between the pretty Irish maid and the handsome Scottish lass. They finally agreed that the dainty maid would carry the day. At least they both got a taste of each other's homeland.

They walked with curiosity through the exotic Midway Plaisance that recreated lands of the Far East with realistic buildings, food, marketplaces, music and native dances.

"Can ya imagine the beautiful dresses that could be made out of this silky gold fabric?" Maggie wondered aloud as she draped the cloth over her arms.

"Well, I can't afford enough for a dress, but could yer make a scarf outta a wee bit?" Mac asked as she gratefully smiled and nodded.

"Are you a seamstress?" a young girl standing next to her in the market asked in a harried voice.

"Yes, I'm a seamstress and dressmaker," Maggie boasted.

"I'm Tatiana. Maybe you can help us." She grabbed Maggie's hand and whisked her to a nearby tent. There she saw a gaggle of young half-dressed Egyptian girls in revealing harem clothing.

"Fatima ripped her pantaloons in the last performance and we can't fix them," the girl said, handing Maggie the garment, needle and thread.

The sheer fabric was tricky to work with, and mending the break in the middle of the pant would take a skilled hand. But as her mother taught her to sew the Irish lace, her needlework was second to none. In just a few minutes, she restored the tear perfectly.

The girls thankfully ushered Mac and Maggie into the tent to watch Little Egypt's show in gratitude.

Much of the gossip about the fair surrounded the risqué costumes and "impure" indigenous dances by the belly dancer named Little Egypt. Her "hoochie coochie" dance was the hit of the fair and equally scorned by the church ladies of the city.

Maggie was entranced at the astonishing way she could twist and move her body. But when she saw the enormous smile on Mac's face, she grabbed his hand in a little fit of jealousy to lead him out of the tent.

"Wait," said a man standing next to the girls. "Do you need a job? We could use a good seamstress." He handed a confused Maggie a card and told her to come back and see him if she was interested. Maggie smiled and put the card in her purse, waving goodbye to the girls.

As dusk rested the sun, they walked hand in hand in a mystical haze.

For the first time, Maggie saw the scene Mrs. Harmon described on opening day of the glorious fireworks display over the basin and the miraculous illumination of thousands of electric light bulbs dancing to shed beams of light over the exhibitions, tricking nighttime back to day.

As they stood together looking at the backdrop of dazzling lights, Mac leaned over and kissed her.

"I hope you'll forgive me, but seeing yer beautiful face lit up in these lights, I couldn't help meself," he said.

Maggie sighed and grinned at him. His kiss was strong, but sweet and gentle, just like him. It was her first kiss and she was lost in overwhelming and strange but wonderful feelings. She liked him and she liked the kiss even more. Everything had her drinking in emotions of intoxication for the fair and for Mac.

For their last event, they queued for the soaring Ferris Wheel, the new engineering phenomenon. Rushing in with crowds of others, they garnered a perfect view through the metal webbed windows in the steel-framed cab car of forty people.

Mac held her around the waist as they watched the sun set on the unique White City and a day they would not soon forget.

"I love yer, Maggie," he whispered in her ear.

"Me too," she said, turning her head to kiss him.

Chapter Seventeen

He said it and she said it. It was out there. After their kiss and love proclamation on the Ferris Wheel, they walked back to Harmon House in a cloud of lovely thoughts.

Mac kissed her again at the door, just like before. Maggie was lost in the rapture of their lips pressing together and his warm, comfortable embrace.

That night, for the first time, she blissfully dreamed of a small house with a garden and a white picket fence with kids laughing and playing in the yard and Mac, as her dutiful husband, kissing her happily on the front porch.

She abruptly awoke when the morning bell rang to begin the day, unsure of her dream or what it meant. Could she be a wife and mother? For now, all she knew was that she loved Mac. That was enough and the rest would come.

"Tell us about the fair," Fiona said at breakfast. Maggie told them of all the wonders she saw, from the Midway and lights to the Ferris Wheel and all the amazing exhibitions.

The rest of the domestics took turns going to the fair so the Harmons would not be left understaffed.

"I can't wait to go next week," Kate said.

"I'll beat you both to the Ferris Wheel," John said. "I want to ride it all day."

"Well now, Mr. Rockefeller, I hope you'll not be wasting your life savings on a child's ride at fifty cents each," Mrs. Donnelly scolded him and ended the discussion.

After everyone left the table, Mrs. Donnelly told Maggie to stay behind.

"How is your fella?" she asked.

Maggie sighed with a beaming grin.

"I love him," Maggie said.

"I know. I saw the stars in your eyes," she said. "I'm glad you found someone that makes your heart sing. I know you've been sour on men. Lord knows there are the devils among them, but some are true angels. Me own father was the salt of the earth. And Fiona's father, God rest him, was the finest man that ever lived."

"I'm not sure what this means. All I know is for right now, I'm just enjoying this fantastic new feeling," Maggie sighed and lightly walked out of the room.

The new maid, Millie, was a young American girl of thirteen from a rural farm outside the city. She was recently orphaned in a fire and she and her remaining siblings were scattered, sent to work in different areas.

Despite her young and innocent appearance, she was pretty with light blonde, almost white hair, blue eyes and a bountiful bustline and slim waist, which made her appear beyond her years.

As soon as Mrs. Donnelly saw her, Maggie heard her instruct Fiona to stay with the girl at all times and keep Mr. Ambrose away from her.

"Stick to her as if you're shackled. She's an innocent lass, just the type the snake likes," Mrs. Donnelly said.

Maggie nodded in agreement. Mr. Ambrose went after every good-looking young female in the house, but she didn't know if the innocent pretty blonde and buxom milkmaid could handle his advances.

But even thoughts of Mr. Ambrose's lechery couldn't dampen her mood. All the next week, Maggie walked on air daydreaming about Mac. But this week they couldn't see each other on Sunday, since the others were going to the fair and she needed to be on duty.

"Please watch Millie like a hawk. Mr. Ambrose has been looking at her like prey, but I've been blocking him," Fiona told Maggie as she was leaving for the fair.

With Mrs. Harmon at a fundraising event and John, Kate, Fiona and Mrs. Donnelly gone for the day, Maggie sat at the servants' kitchen table to keep an eye out and write to her mother.

Suzanne Rudd Hamilton

Dearest Mother,

Seeing the fair with me own eyes was the grandest thing I have or will ever have in me life. I wish ya could've seen it too. I've included a couple picture postcards for ya, but they don't compare to the real thing.

It's the most beautiful and wondrous place in the world and a magical time for me. I will never forget it as long as I live.

And that building full of marvelous new inventions to make life better made me see things in a new light. It showed me people can do anything if they put their minds to it. Like you always say, the milk doesn't pour itself.

I've been afraid of stepping out of my station and also scared to let a man control me. Now I see that nothing can do that, unless I let it.

I wrote you before about me Scotsman, David McIntyre. I call him Mac. We went to the fair together and been seeing a lot of each other. And he kissed me and I kissed him back.

Mac and I are in a lovely place. He's a good man and he cares for me deeply and I him. For the first time, I can see meself in that house with kids in the yard and maybe even see my seamstress dreams coming true too. It's all in front of me for the taking and I feel like I can grab it. Everything is possible. I believe it now.

Your darling Maggie

When she was done with the letter, she went out to put it out for the mail and saw Mac coming up the walk.

"I'm glad to see ya, I am, but what are ya doing here?" Maggie asked.

"I couldn't stay away. I know you're working, but I felt like I would die if I didn't see your face even for a second and bring yer some daisies to brighten your day," Mac said.

Maggie smiled and looked at the daisies, then looked up at Mac and fixed his collar.

"Ya beast of a man, ya unhinge me in me very soul," she laughed.

"Can I get a small peck to tide me over?" he asked, puckering his lips.

Maggie quickly kissed him and laughed, touching his cheek.

"Now be on with ya before someone sees."

"I'll be at the pub later, if yer can get away," he said and threw her a kiss goodbye.

She returned to the house grinning happily, smelling the daisies. She went into the kitchen to get an empty milk bottle to put them in and saw Millie in the corner with her dress pulled down to the waist and her breasts exposed with Mr. Ambrose's hands cupping them with an evil lecherous grin on his face.

The girl was not struggling, but she was terrified. She looked right into Maggie's eyes for help.

It was like history repeating itself, but this time, she would not count to three, calm down or leave. Maggie went into a rage and started hitting Mr. Ambrose with the daisies in her hand.

"I'll thank ya to take your grimy little hands off that poor young lass right now!" Maggie yelled.

Frightened, Millie ran away crying and left Maggie screaming at Mr. Ambrose.

"How dare ya make every girl in this house your private hoochie coochie show with your unwanted advances, all to do the bidding of your lustful devilish ways and dark soul!" she said and then turned around to leave.

"You Irish trash, you don't tell me what I can and can't do in this household."

Mr. Ambrose erupted. He grabbed Maggie, dragging her to the corner and pinned her against the wall to grope her breasts.

Her Irish temper was at its breaking point. She seethed at him, mustered all her strength and ire and smacked him across the face as hard as she could, causing him to fall backward.

She ran straight up to her room, horrified with rushes of tears streaming down her face. With the adrenaline rush, she pushed her bed against the door and sat on the floor, holding her legs and crying uncontrollably.

"That awful man. That horrible devil of a man himself," she bawled.

Everything she thought shattered into pieces. That she could rise above her station, that she could be a seamstress and a mother; it was all gone in a few moments.

All the anger about what happened to Caroline, Molly, Millie and her mother flooded back at once like a raging river. She wept for all of them, stuck in situations that made them vulnerable to the lewd desires and shameless intentions of any man who forced themselves on others.

A few hours later, she heard a knock at the door.

"Maggie, me girl. It's Mrs. Donnelly. Let me in. I brought tea. I'm so angry I nearly steamed it meself."

Maggie stood up, moved the bed slightly, and slowly opened the door to let her in, afraid of the consequences that lie on the other side.

"I'm sorry you're upset. Mr. Ambrose made some claims and Millie told me what happened. I've come to hear it from your lips," she said softly and handed her the cup.

Still shaking, Maggie put the cup to her mouth and sipped it between sobs, trying to get her composure.

"Oh, Mrs. Donnelly, I'm so sorry. I took my eyes off her for a wee bit and he was having his way with the poor babe. She looked at me like she saw the very devil himself.

I couldn't let him hurt her. Then he got randy with me and tried the same thing. I couldn't help my Irish—I gave it right back to him but good," Maggie stated, wiping her wet face."

"I understand. I've been in service a long time now and seen men of all stations try to push their will on young girls and women. I envy you for standing up, but it won't be without cost," Mrs. Donnelly explained.

"I'm not sorry. I stand by what I did. Me mother warned me about me temper, but I've seen the underside of this and couldn't let it happen again. To live a life where even your body is not your own is doomed to Hades itself," Maggie stated, holding up her head with renewed confidence.

"Mr. Ambrose has already spoken to the missus. I'll speak to her too, but you know how it's done," Mrs. Donnelly said, lowering her head, then left the room.

Maggie knew what would happen and started packing her things. Women did not stand up to men, especially in service. There was a hierarchical order and you didn't counter those above and definitely didn't attack them.

A little while later, Fiona came to her door in tears.

"Me mother says the missus wants to see ya," Fiona said and firmly hugged Maggie.

Maggie wiped her face, took a deep breath and went to Mrs. Harmon's room, rapping on the door.

"Come in, Donegal," she said solemnly.

"I understand there was an incident. Mrs. Donnelly explained everything. Please don't misunderstand me—I am aware of Mr. Ambrose's proclivities. Mrs. Ambrose knows as well. Men can be difficult creatures, but it's up to women to rise above their prurient instincts and keep our temperament for our own survival. We cannot give in to their actions and react with our own aggressions."

Maggie looked at her directly for a minute in silence and measured her response.

"I understand, ma'am, but if rising up means getting stomped into the mud over and over, I wonder if we will ever be able to grow. The price is too high," she said in a quiet but dignified voice.

"I'll leave on me own, but as me mother always said, 'What a sober man has in his heart, the drunk has on his lips.' And for meself I'll say that those who sit by knowing may as well drink just the same. And me name is Maggie Donnelly."

Maggie marched out and went directly back to her room, where Fiona, Kate and Millie were all crying, waiting for her.

"I'm so sorry, Maggie. It's all my fault," Millie said.

"Nonsense, 'tis that devil Mr. Ambrose. I'll have a mind to smack him one meself," Fiona said with her fists up.

"How did it feel to hit him?" Kate asked.

"All I felt was ire. I'm not saying I was right or wrong, but I'm hoping now that he got a little back at him, he'll think again," Maggie said and hugged each of them.

She picked up her bag, glanced around the room, and said goodbye to her beloved sewing machine. Once again, a man's visceral needs and cruel intentions came between her and a beloved sewing machine.

Maggie walked down the stairs to find everyone at the door to see her off. Everyone except Mr. and Mrs. Ambrose.

She smiled at them warmly and made her way to the door. Even though she was treated unjustly, she knew they thought she was right. That helped. She would miss them all.

"Oh and Mr. Ambrose," she called out. "As me Irish mother says, may the cat eat ya and may the devil eat the cat."

On the other side of the door, Maggie stopped and held her breath for a moment. Once again, she didn't know what she was going to do or where she would go, but this time, she wasn't alone. She knew what she needed—to see Mac.

Walking briskly to the pub, she found Mac at the bar drinking and laughing with his mates.

He smiled and waved when he saw her enter. She ran to him and began to weep on his shoulder.

"There, there now, lass, what brought this on?" he asked and gently wiped her tears away with his finger.

She explained what happened and he held her tight.

"The boys and I can take care of him. Yer just say the word and we'll off with him good," he firmly said to her.

"No, I'd not soil your knuckles with the likes of that gurrier," she stated with assurance.

"Well, I don't know what that's Irish for, but I bet it's not good. As me mother used to say, men are like bagpipes—no sound comes from them until they are full. And some never get full of their want, no matter what it is."

Maggie looked up at him with pure love in her eyes. She knew no matter what she thought of other men, that he was a good one. He was the right one.

"Well, there's one thing left to do. I was thinking on it anyway, but now is as good as any. We need to get married right away. Will yer have me?" he asked with a smile.

Maggie gazed into his bright blue marble eyes and all the doubts and fears melted away. She loved him. That was all she needed to know.

"Is now too soon?" She laughed, then grabbed his beer and drank it in one swallow.

He let out a hearty laugh and kissed her as everyone in the bar cheered.

Despite the hour, Mac and Maggie couldn't wait to be wed, so they walked to her church to wake the priest and see if he could marry them.

They found Father Morley in the chapel, starting to snuffing the candles.

"Father, pardon the interruption, but can ya marry us right away?" she asked with a hopeful look on her face.

The priest stared for a few moments at Maggie and then at Mac and then back again.

"Are you sure?" he asked, examining their faces again.

"Aye, your grace. I've loved this woman from the moment my eyes met her beautiful green eyes. She's like no one I ever knew and I want to be with her always," Mac said sincerely.

A tear of joy streamed down Maggie's face as he spoke.

"I can see you feel the same way, my dear," the priest smiled. "So, I guess there's no time like the present."

She opened her purse and took out the lace handkerchief her mother had made for her and held it in her hands to keep her close to her heart.

Maggie and Mac kneeled at the altar in the dimmed candlelight as the priest spoke the marriage vows. Their eyes lingered as they gazed at each other and held hands, mesmerized in the light of their love. Minutes later, they were man and wife.

Overwhelmed with emotion, she dried her happy tears with her soaked handkerchief. When she went to her purse to get another, she saw the card from Little Egypt's manager at the fair.

It was a sign. Everything was going to be fine.

Chapter Eighteen

That night they went back to Mac's rooming house.

He picked her up in one smooth motion and carried her over the threshold, both laughing quietly so as not to disturb anyone.

"I'm sorry my room is so small. Yer deserve better," he said.

"It has you, so it's perfect." She smiled and kissed him.

He placed her on the bed and lit the candles. In the amber glow of the room, they sat on the bed staring into each other's eyes.

"Now, I don't want yer to be embarrassed or feel unsure. I can wait until yer say the word," he said sweetly.

Maggie focused her eyes on his and smiled. In that moment, full of unrelenting love for him, she never wanted anything more in her life.

"Ready," she said and kissed him full on the lips, pushing him backward on the bed.

The entire night was like being lost in a dream. He gently caressed her all over and kissed her lovingly. She felt as if her skin melted each time his lips touched it.

With her finger, she circled his face and neck down to his hairy bare chest, studying the deep definition of his muscles for the first time. She entangled her fingers in his red chest hair.

He carefully unbuttoned her dress and pulled it down, hesitating at her underdress and corset, blushing as he looked at her, his eyes asking for permission.

She smiled at him and chuckled at his sweetness, then loosened her corset and yanked down her underdress.

As she held him closely, she could feel his body tremble in anticipation.

Without reservation, she relinquished herself to him, body and soul, their sweaty skin binding them together forever. They were one. It was a freedom she never felt before—total immersion with another person.

The next morning, beams of sunlight careened through the window and danced on the wall, awakening her.

She rubbed her eyes to ensure she was awake and saw Mac lying next to her. Smiling, she twisted his red-orange hair through her fingers and touched his cheek. It wasn't a dream. She was married.

Maggie kissed him on the cheek.

"Awaken, me husband, and greet the new day," she said with a chuckle.

He opened his sapphire blue eyes and looked right at her and smiled.

"Madainn mhath, me wife," he said and kissed her gently.

He rose from the bed and stepped to the dresser in all his nakedness.

Paying no attention to her own bareness, Maggie blushed and turned her eyes at first, but then smiled and looked straight on to see his chiseled body in the full light.

Her eyes followed his every move as he went to the dresser and pulled a small wooden box from a drawer.

"This is me grandmother's wedding ring. It worked for them for fifty years, so I'll bet it's good luck." He gazed at her lovingly and slid the ring on her finger.

Maggie looked down at the ring and grinned. The band was antique gold and black, embossed with tiny swirls of ivy. And in the center lay a luminous emerald stone shining in the sunlight.

"The emerald is as bright and radiant as your eyes," he said, then smiled and kissed her. "Oh, and I don't think I mentioned. Me granny was an Irish lass."

She thrust her arms around his neck and kissed him, dragging him back into the bed.

After he left for work, Maggie sat in the bed beaming in the afterglow of their love, with her head in the clouds.

A day ago, she was in love. Now she was a married woman. She happily beamed and stretched with her arms wide, drinking in the joy of her new life.

She put her underdress on over her head and busied herself around the room, making the bed, cleaning up the clothes and dusting the furniture.

For now, at least, this was their home and she was going to make it cleaner than all the homes she served. But it was a different feeling—she was cleaning her home for herself and her new husband. This time, it wasn't just a chore, it was done with love.

After she finished, she looked around the room with pride and got dressed. She grabbed her purse and looked at the card from the Little Egypt tent. It said:

Edgar Kagan, Manager

If they were going to get a house of their own, she needed to get a position and earn some money too. After a life in service, she knew she was a hard worker and could put her skills to use.

She put on her straw hat and traveling suit and walked down to the fairgrounds with purpose. She showed the card to the security guard at the gate and he directed her to the back gate near the Midway. Once there, she handed the card to another guard and told him a man named Kagan asked her to call.

The guard let her in the back gate and pointed toward Cairo Street, where she met Little Egypt and her dancers just a week before.

The Midway looked different now. Instead of a wonder of amazement, she saw a busy street with people bustling and trying to do their work to prepare for the day's crowds. She also saw the crammed spaces in the backstages of the exhibits on the street.

She walked into the tent to find the men hanging the lights and the girls in regular day clothes sitting there talking. It was like pulling back the curtain and seeing the reality behind the fantasy world.

"You came back. I am so glad!" Tatiana said as soon as she saw Maggie. She ran to greet her.

The dancers immediately gathered around Maggie. They were all a little shorter than her, with dark eyes and luxurious long black hair and silky tan skin. She showed them her wedding ring and left them swooning with the romantic tale of her whirlwind wedding.

"Look, Kagan, the seamstress is back. Her name is Maggie," Tatiana told him.

Kagan was a shorter, stout man with a stubbly face. He wore a black suit with a big bowler hat, which obscured most of his head. He hobbled toward her, encircled in a cloud of cigar smoke, and blew a puff of cigar smoke into the air.

"Let's talk," he said in a raspy voice. He waved for her to follow him into another part of the tent.

"You know what you're doing. These girls constantly rip everything. We can use you. When can you start? Pays $40 per week until the end of the fair."

Maggie's jaw nearly dropped to the ground. She didn't even make that in a month as a lady's maid.

"I can start now," she said.

"Good, go find the girls and see what they need done," he said and walked away.

Maggie excitedly went back to see Tatiana and the girls. It was her first paid job as a seamstress. For the first time, she was being rewarded for her sewing skills alone.

"I'm going to be helping ya with your costumes," Maggie told Tatiana. "What do ya need?"

As soon as the words left her mouth, she was barraged by a collection of scarves, pantaloons and vests along with comments from the girls in a variety of languages and broken English.

Tatiana must have seen Maggie's look of confusion and shouted something in a different language. In an instant, all the girls dropped their garments and left the room.

"My apology, they are very happy to have your expert help. Most of them do not speak English, so I will get a list of everything that is needed," Tatiana said.

"Thank ya so much. I just couldn't understand what they were saying. Where can I work?" Maggie asked and gathered the previously tossed garments in her arms.

Tatiana smiled and waved for Maggie to follow her into an adjacent tent where the girls dressed. It was messy, with clothes and shoes strewn all over. A big wooden table lined the wall filled with beads and makeup.

Maggie looked at all the materials used to paint faces and chuckled, grateful she didn't have to use any of that.

At the end of the room, she saw a small table and chair with bolts of material stacked on and around it.

"Here you are. I will come back with the list," Tatiana said, smiling.

Maggie saw a big box in the corner and dropped the garments in it, then moved it to the edge of the small table.

Then she unbuttoned her jacket, put it on the back of the chair, rolled up her sleeves and began moving the bolts of fabric to a pile against the tent wall. After moving a few bolts, she uncovered a wonderful surprise—a sewing machine.

It wasn't new and shiny, but it worked and she was relieved to have it, considering all the labor ahead of her.

Tatiana returned with another woman. She was shorter, with long black hair and oval eyes. Her face was painted with various colors to accentuate her eyes, lips and cheeks.

"Maggie, this is Fatima," Tatiana said. "You sewed her pantaloons."

"They call me Little Egypt, but you may call me Fatima," she said to Maggie and bowed her head. "You will make me a spectacular costume for my show?"

She bowed her head again and left, leaving Maggie even more confused.

"What kind of costume does she need?" Maggie asked.

Tatiana smiled and handed her the list. "You saw the show before. Watch again today and make her something shiny and flowy."

Maggie watched a show or two in between mending to get an idea of what Fatima needed. After the shock of the first show and meeting the girls in person, she had a new appreciation for the art of the dances and was brimming with ideas for new costumes.

She made a few notes and finished sewing for the day. It was near dusk, and Mac would wonder where she was, so she walked back to the rooming house as quickly as she could.

When she entered, she saw him huddled over the fireplace, stirring a pot poised on a spit.

"Well, there's me bride. I was wondering if I dreamt the whole thing. And then I saw how clean the room was and knew it wasn't me," he laughed.

Maggie took her jacket and hat off, gave him a lasting kiss, and hugged him tight.

"If that's how yer going to greet me every day, I'm going to like this marriage," he said, laughing and holding her. "What has yer so tickled? It is me kisses?"

"Yes, but today I went back to those people we met at the fair. The ones I helped. And they hired me to be a seamstress. Finally, I will be paid for sewing, designing and mending," she said kissing him again.

"Now that's a fine thing to keep yer occupied for now," Mac said.

"Yes, and they will pay me $40 per week," she said.

Mac dropped the stirring spoon on the floor.

"Per week?"

"Yes, isn't that wonderful? We can save up and get an apartment in no time." She smiled and picked up the spoon and wiped it off, then started stirring the soup.

Mac sat down at the small table and stared at the floor in silence.

Maggie put the soup in bowls and placed them on the table. Then she grabbed a few slices of bread and sat down.

"I'll make sure to come home in time to make dinner tomorrow," she said. "It was very hectic, being the first day."

"Hmm," he said and ate his soup without a word.

They made love again that night and fell asleep in each other's arms. The warm feeling of their marital bed was a comfort she never expected and would not want to be without.

Bursting with excitement, Maggie woke early before the morning light and gazed in amazement at Mac and the fortune of her new life. She wanted to share it with her mother.

Dearest Mother,

You are probably surprised why I'm posting another letter so soon, but I had to write and tell you of my bliss.

It all came to an end with Mr. Ambrose, and me Irish got the best of me—as usual. He was taking advantage of a poor wee girl and I gave it to him and good. This time me fists went first.

But something wonderful came out of it. Mac and I got married and are now living as man and wife. I know it seems rushed, but I love him and have never been happier.

We're both Catholic and felt it was important, so we made sure to be married in the church by the priest, if you're wondering, so we did it up right.

I wish you were there with me, but I kept your handkerchief in my hand, soes I felt your warm loving eyes looking upon me.

And I got a new job as a seamstress right off and will be making good money. I know you said you don't want anything from me but joy, and we need to save for an apartment, but I'll be sending you some when I can. You can buy a new hat or some gloves for yourself.

    I hope you'll be glad for me. It was a quick one, it was, but he's a grand man and I love him a lot. I know we'll be happy always.

    Your darling married daughter, Maggie (Mrs. David McIntyre)

Chapter Nineteen

The next few months at the fair were a pleasure. It was hard work, as Kagan was right—the girls did tear their clothes a lot. But more than that, when they saw the costume she made for Fatima, each of the girls tried to persuade Maggie to make something special for them.

She didn't mind and loved the challenges of adding some fringe, scarves or beads here and there. It was a cheery place to work. She looked forward to each workday like never before, even at Windermere.

Cairo Street became her neighborhood, where she would banter with the merchants and vendors and learn about their countries and cultures. Everything around her inspired creativity. The lines and curves of the buildings, colorful native costumes, vibrant chants and dances, and the array of fabrics, food and wares were inspiring.

The girls were bubbly all the time, laughing and humming and working at the bustling fair. And listening to the exuberant crowds applauding their act was jubilant.

Backstage, the girls continually showered her with praise about her work. Even though people admired and complimented her work before, this was a true appreciation she never felt.

She enjoyed her freedom of exploration on Cairo Street and absorbed everything she saw about their way of life. But she was disheartened by the underbelly of the crippling work and unpleasant conditions, with many people sleeping on cots or bedrolls on the floor of the same room.

It was an unfortunate reality of the fair that she recognized, but couldn't change, so she tried to engage with them as much as the language barrier would allow and learn as much as she could.

Each day, Maggie cleaned their room before work and hurried home to cook whatever she could in their fireplace. As meat was expensive and baking was not easy with open flame cooking, she became a bit of a gourmet with soups and stews. Sometimes Mac would bring a fish or two from the lake if he was working nearby and could leave a line in the water.

A few times, she brought small morsels home from the fair to spice up the meals with special treats. She learned a few tricks from some of the vendors about using exotic flavorings and zest. But both she and Mac had very simple palates of breads, meats, potatoes and vegetables, bred from birth in their home countries.

Married life suited Maggie. She and Mac spent the night hours together sitting by the fire reading to each other, strolling in the moonlight hand in hand and making love every night only to fall asleep entwined.

On Saturday nights, they went to the pub to play games and meet with friends. And on their day off, they went to church and then walked around exploring the city and searching for an apartment in a nice neighborhood.

It was a cozy and relaxed life, giving her a feeling of warmth and home, something she hadn't experienced since she left Ireland.

Finally, one of Mac's friends told them of an available apartment in his building, so they visited it after church one Sunday.

The moment they walked in the door, Maggie's eyes lit up with excitement.

It was a small one-bedroom apartment with a sitting room, bedroom, and kitchenette. They would have to share a bath with only two other apartments, unlike the wait in line single bath at the rooming house.

The building was within walking distance of the fair for Maggie and close to the streetcar, so it could take Mac to any job location in the city.

When they visited, she noticed the wonderful aromas seeping under every door each night and the joyous sound, full of children's laughter.

Maggie was a little worried about the rent, as the fair would be ending in a few months and she didn't know how long it would take to get more work.

"Don't worry, darling; like good Scots, our miserly ways serve us well. We have a little can of money and can use it to enjoy some space. And with this kitchen, yer can cook something other than stew." He laughed and placed his arm around her to put her at ease.

Soon they moved into the meagerly furnished apartment with a bed, table, wardrobe and small sofa. In the rooming house, they had to read in bed or on the floor by the fire, but now they could snuggle up together on the sofa.

Maggie cleaned and spruced up the place for a few days to make the apartment homey. The first Sunday after they moved, she splurged on a small chicken and some apples, sugar and flour to make a pie in their stove.

They didn't have an icebox, but the kitchen included a pie safe, so she could make a whole chicken, pie and loaf of bread and save any left to keep for the next day.

She started the bread mixture the night before and put it in the safe to rise. Then after church, she baked the bread and pie, still using a fireplace spit for the chicken.

Mac went to bring home some firewood and returned with a beautiful bouquet of wildflowers to brighten up their table.

"It's been a while since I brought yer a bunch of flowers," he said, grinning. "I know how much yer love them."

Maggie was near tears at his sweet gesture. Looking around at their new home, she felt the world was complete. And despite her worries, she was happy to have her own home.

October came quickly. She counted down each day until the planned fair closing on the 30th. As the final day drew nearer, Maggie and her friends at the fair were saddened by the end of the short adventure.

A few days before the closing, Maggie wandered down Cairo Street and the Midway to ensure she said goodbye to everyone she'd met. Since they came from other parts of the world, she knew she'd never see them or experience their cultures again.

With the long tedious hours and crowded and harsh accommodations with little room for the indigenous people who were constantly on public display, some of the people were more than happy to return to their homeland.

But Tatiana and the dancing girls and some others Maggie befriended were sad to leave. They relished the eye-opening experiences of coming to America, even though it was only the America inside the gates of the fair.

"This was the world to us. Here, we see different people and places and learned about their countries. I will never see their lands. And people are so happy to see us," Tatiana told Maggie.

Two days before the closing of the fair, Kagan called Maggie into his office. Fatima was already waiting there.

"Kid, Fatima wants you to go on the road with her, as her costume mistress. It pays $75 per week, all expenses paid," he said with the cigar hanging from his mouth.

"I would really enjoy having you with us, Maggie," Fatima urged.

Maggie was shocked. The money. The opportunity. The things she would see. It was the offer of a lifetime that a single Maggie would have considered wonderful, but married Maggie had to turn it down.

"I thank ya so much for the offer. It's a great compliment and I appreciate it more than ya know. But I'm a married woman and I couldn't leave my husband like that," Maggie said.

"Maybe I could write you when I need new costumes and you could send them to me?" Fatima asked.

"Oh, I would welcome that. Please write to me," Maggie said with enthusiasm. She wrote her address on a slip of paper and gave it to her.

As she walked past the front gates, she heard Mayor Carter Harrison giving the closing address for the exposition, with local crowds gathered to hear him speak. The closing ceremonies wouldn't have the pomp and circumstance of the opening but promised at least the fair would go out with a bang.

She both dreaded and awaited her final day at the fair, as it would be mixed with the sadness of leaving, but the joy of the final festivities and rumored fireworks display.

The next morning, Maggie and Mac woke to the sound of a newsboy yelling, "The mayor is dead! Read all about it! The mayor is dead!"

She looked out the window and saw crowds gathering around the boy, grabbing papers. People were gasping with shock and awe that made some ladies scream and faint, while others cried.

Mac quickly dressed and ran down to get a newspaper and find out what happened.

"People on the street and in the building are all talking about it. He was shot last night in his home," Mac said when he returned.

Carter Harrison was known as the mayor of the common man and much beloved by the people. Some people mourned him, and others were concerned by a violent crime that couldn't even protect the mayor of the city in his own home.

In deference to the mayor, the fair's closing ceremonies were canceled in favor of a public memorial service held instead.

The tragic event laid a dreary cloak of sadness on the Columbian Exposition, which had been the jewel in the city's crown.

Suzanne Rudd Hamilton

As she walked down Cairo Street, she saw everything closing up and being dismantled a little bit at a time.

It was so sad that an event that began with so much hope and glorious celebration went out with a dark cloud hanging over it.

When she went to the tent, Kagan told her that there would be no shows that day and she could go home. He handed her money for her final week of work and she bid tearful goodbyes to all the girls.

"Don't worry, Maggie. We will write to you and I hope you can make us more beautiful things," Tatiana said with her typical cheerful smile.

Maggie hugged her tight.

"Thanks for being a ray of sunshine every day. Have a beautiful life," she said.

As she walked out the gates toward home, she wondered what kind of life Tatiana and the other girls would have. Traveling around giving hoochie coochie shows for leering men may be just another kind of prison, just like her life in domestic service work. No freedom and no respect.

She couldn't wait to get home to Mac. With him, she knew her life would be much better than the girls on the road.

When he came home, she told him everything she saw on the Midway and Cairo Street.

"Aye, 'tis a darn shame. And me boss told me today that we are taking everything down and demolishing all the buildings, so it will be a park again," Mac said.

Tears streamed down her face, just thinking of the wondrous White City reduced to rubble and carted away.

"Mac, I don't want to go back to service work. I want to try to get work as a seamstress," Maggie blurted out.

"I'd be pleased if yer you didn't work at all. I'd prefer my wife to be at home, but for now, yer do what makes yer happy," he assured her.

For the next few weeks, Maggie read the paper and visited dress shops in town to find work.

Each day she felt tired and disappointed. She knew Mac said she didn't have to work, but she needed to work to earn money so they wouldn't have to go back to the rooming house.

When he came home that night, she was lying in bed crying.

"Ah, me beauty, what ails you?" he softly asked, gently stroking her hair.

"I'm frustrated that I can't find work making clothes. It's making me all tired and weepy. I made ya some cottage pie, but I'm not eating," she said.

"Yer haven't been hungry for a while. Sure yer ok?" he asked.

Suzanne Rudd Hamilton

As soon as the words left his mouth, Maggie's mind began to race. Caroline was sleepy, cried all the time and wouldn't eat when she was in the family way.

What if she was with child?

Chapter Twenty

Maggie was in the family way. Days after her revelation, she was fairly certain, but to make sure, she went over to Harmon House to ask Mrs. Donnelly.

Since she left the manor, she saw Fiona and Mrs. Donnelly at church every Sunday, but she needed a woman's wisdom and couldn't wait. She asked John to have Mrs. Donnelly step outside and not mention her name.

Her surrogate mother was glad but surprised to see her. She looked at Maggie curiously, hoping nothing was wrong.

"Me girl, I'm happy to see ya. Are you ok? Something's different about ya," Mrs. Donnelly looked pensively at Maggie."

"That's what I thought. I'm tired, weepy and can't eat a bite. I think I'm...?"

She didn't wait for Maggie to finish. Her eyes lit up and she hugged Maggie with a jubilant chuckle in her voice.

"Oh, me girl, you made me the happiest woman in the place. There's going to be a wee wee bairn."

Mrs. Donnelly wanted to invite Maggie in to discuss her news, but as Mr. and Mrs. Ambrose still ran the household, Maggie was unwelcome. She thanked Mrs. Donnelly and kissed her on the cheek to say goodbye. They agreed to discuss the happy news more on Sunday.

Maggie smiled on the way back to her apartment as it started to sink in. She was going to have a babe of her very own.

She spent the rest of the day milling about their home, cleaning and cooking to make a special dinner for Mac—Scottish meat pies.

Spending a life in domestic service outside the kitchen, however, did not make her an expert cook.

She tried her best to make his mother's Scottish meat pies, based only on Mac's description of the ingredients. He said it was his was his favorite meal.

When Mac came home, the apartment was dimly lit with only a few candles for atmosphere.

With a brimming grin, she presented him with the meat pie.

"I've heard ya talk about Scottish meat pies so much, I thought it would be a special treat," she said proudly.

Although he tried to hide it, his expression said it all.

"This is new," he said, desperately trying to hold back laughter. "I've never had a whole one like this."

When he cut into it, the loose meat filling ran out of the center onto the plate. It was meat stew put into a pie crust.

With Maggie's emotions on edge and her tear prone condition, she could no longer hold back the burst dam and began to cry.

"Don't cry. I love it. Yum," he said with a glint in his eyes, gobbling the meat mixture. "Yer didn't know they were supposed to be small pies."

Maggie laughed out loud at the silly sight of him shoveling the meat in his mouth to please her.

"Ya daft man. But no sweeter one ever lived," she said and kissed him. "I'm not weeping for the pie. "I'm going to have a baby."

Mac was so surprised he choked and spit out his food onto the plate.

"Now?" he asked, panicked.

"No, ya kind fool, it will take a few months," she laughed.

Once he took hold of his senses, he sprang up from the chair and held her tightly and then, thinking of the baby he loosened his grip and kissed her long and hard.

"Thank yer, Maggie. This is a bonnie day. I will be a father!" he yelled happily out the window.

"Yes, it's a grand day at that," she laughed, watching him.

Suzanne Rudd Hamilton

Dearest Mother,

I have wonderful news. You will soon be a gran! I'm in the family way. Mac is over the moon. He keeps asking me what he can do for me and treating me like a queen when he comes home.

Of course, when he leaves, I do the cooking, cleaning and washing as usual. I wonder if he thinks it all happens by magic.

He's put his stubborn Scottish foot down about me working while expecting the wee bairn. I don't want to go against me husband's wishes, but he has no idea of all the things a baby needs.

But for right now, I'll heed his wishes. I'm making all the layette clothes and wee blankets. And Mac started to make a bassinet that rocks the baby to sleep.

I've never been so excited for anything in me life. I think back to when Moira and Liam were born. I was so proud and happy to love and care for them, but they were never me own. This one will be a McIntyre, half-Irish and half-Scottish. God help it.

May the good Lord bless this baby and keep him from my temper and his stubbornness. A child who has both will make a tough way in this world.

I won't tell Mac this, but secretly I hope for a girl. Those days we had together were so special. I want to try to pass on all the good thoughts and advice ya gave to me own daughter.

I know the old Irish saying about having a good friend, but I'm changing it. I say a good mother is like a four-leaf clover—hard to find and lucky to have.

All I can hope is to do half as well as you.

Your darling daughter plus one, Maggie

Several months went by and the fairgrounds were beginning to revert to the empty and green Jackson Park.

Maggie and Mac wandered by once a week for a while, but as she grew bigger, they stopped.

She felt connected to the fair. So many good memories that paved her future were wrapped up in the fair; it saddened her to see it end.

Before the final building came down, Maggie told Mac she wanted to lay eyes on it again. As they walked past the old fairgrounds, Maggie wept as she saw the rubble and vast emptiness of what once was a vibrant and wondrous place.

"I think the wee babe makes yer weep at the very drop of a hat," he teased and dried her tears lovingly with his hand.

"I know, but it changed my life," she said, blubbering and reaching in her purse for her handkerchief.

Suzanne Rudd Hamilton

Two months later, her baby boy screamed his way into the world with piles of blazing red hair. They called him Davey.

Mac was so happy he bought a box of cheap cigars and handed them out to everyone he met.

Maggie was finally a mother. She rocked her baby in the beautiful bassinet Mac made, all the while singing Irish lullabies and telling him the tale of Tír na nÓg.

She wrote her mother of the birth and how proud she and Mac were to have their own family.

Several weeks later, right before Davey's christening, she received a letter from New York. It was from Caroline.

When she saw the post, a lump stuck in her throat. She knew, after all these years, something must have happened to prompt her to write.

Dear Maggie,

You must know something is amiss since I'm writing to you.

I'm sorry to tell you that Katherine has gone on. My mother was beside herself and couldn't stand to write you this terrible news.

If it's any consolation, she went peacefully in her sleep.

I'm so sorry for this and many things.

My mother told me you are married. I'm very happy for you and I wish you all the best.

Carrie

When Mac returned from work, Maggie was inconsolable. Her mother was not an old woman, but service work was hard and took the years off faster.

She held Davey and cried for days. She didn't know if the message of her grandchild made it to her mother, but Maggie decided that either way, she knew.

Davey's christening went as planned. Maggie believed that the baby needed to be brought to God to protect him from the devil, so it could not be delayed. But what should have been a joyous occasion was dampened by a veil of deep sadness.

Mrs. Donnelly and Fiona were bursting with pride over little Davey. And as they were her only family in America, Maggie made Mrs. Donnelly the baby's godmother. Having them there made Maggie miss her mother a little less.

After the christening, Mac took Davey and went into the back of the church while Maggie prayed and lit a candle for her dear mother.

"Dear God, ya have me mother with ya now, so you're lucky. As me mother said, those we love don't go away, they walk beside us every day. I know she'll help your hand to guide me as a mother and keep little Davey from harm. I wish I could have put me mother at peace meself, but I will have to say me goodbyes through you," Maggie said with tears streaming down her face.

She prayed in silence for a little while longer and then got up, dried her tears and turned to Mac and Davey.

Mac held her hand and squeezed it tight, looking into her sullen eyes, helpless to ease her pain.

"That's done now," she said and they walked out the big wooden church doors hand in hand and closed them behind them.

Chapter Twenty-One

The next couple years were lean ones. Just as she was getting used to being a mother, Maggie had another baby, a little girl called Katie—Katherine after her devoted mother. And the apartment began to get a little crowded.

Mac found work easily, but it was tough to feed a family on a mason's wage.

A few times a year, Fatima would write and send her money to make a costume. That helped, but it wasn't a lot.

Maggie always told Mac she was making something for a friend to soothe his bruised pride and Scottish stubbornness about her working.

Every day, Maggie took Davey and Katie for walks in the pram, while she tried to sell pieces she made to dressmakers and entice them to employ her.

Even with two babies and no sewing machine, Maggie was an expert seamstress and could make anything.

Mrs. Donnelly and Fiona encouraged her to write Mrs. Harmon for a reference to open a few doors. Perhaps out of guilt or obligation, but mostly from respect for her work, Mrs. Harmon gladly gave her a glowing reference, touting her design and sewing prowess and flawless work ethic. Mrs. Harmon even ordered some pieces from her.

And given Mrs. Harmon's society status, it opened a few doors, but after seeing two babies in tow, most dressmakers kindly took her card and said they would let her know. And they never did.

Since she reconnected with Mrs. Harmon, Mrs. Donnelly and Fiona were free to visit when they had an hour or two off. They no longer had to sneak around anymore, seeing her and the children only at church.

Mrs. Donnelly loved playing with Davey and Katie. She brought them treats and loved them like her own grandchildren. Maggie relished the time she spent with them having tea and chatting. Fiona always made Maggie laugh like no one else.

And she needed a break at times. Her littlens were the joy of her life and she loved her alone time with Mac too, but in the daily grind, a little time with female companionship was a priceless commodity.

"I know if these dressmakers would give me a chance, I could make some wonderful pieces for them, but all they see is a mother of two and think I won't be able to keep up," Maggie said, venting her frustration.

Mrs. Donnelly looked at Maggie and set down her tea with defiance.

"Well, I'll not have those snooty women look down on my girl. You can do better than me and your dear departed mother, bless her soul. You can have what we couldn't. And so you will. You show them," Mrs. Donnelly proclaimed, standing to her feet.

A few days later, Mrs. Donnelly agreed to stay with Davey and Katie, while Maggie visited a shop Mrs. Harmon recommended.

To ensure better success, Mrs. Donnelly spoke with Mrs. Harmon and she agreed to meet Maggie at the shop to make introductions in person.

Maggie nervously wore a dress she augmented with various techniques. But with her limited means, she could only showcase them in affordable muslin and cotton and had no pictures of the pieces she made in the past for Mrs. Harmon, Fatima and Caroline.

She stood outside the shop waiting nervously as Mrs. Harmon's carriage pulled up. She was playing her best and final hand with all her cards on the table. If this didn't work, she would have to fold.

To Maggie's surprise, Mrs. Harmon was wearing a suit with the herringbone vest she made for her and brought along John, carrying a box with the ballgown Maggie crafted for her to wear to one of the fair galas.

Mrs. Harmon entered the dress shop to a warm welcome with the proprietor immediately coming to greet her. Maggie noted how different it was from the cool reception she received at many other dressmakers in town.

"Madame Bouvier. May I introduce Mrs. McIntyre. She was my personal modiste, but I sadly lost her to love and marriage. She's interested in collaborating with an established custom dressmaker. You were the first one I recommended," Mrs. Harmon stated and turned to wink privately at Maggie.

Madame Bouvier quietly examined the gown and glanced at what Mrs. Harmon and Maggie were wearing.

"But of course, Mrs. Harmon. The recommendation of a woman of your taste is impeccable, but I'm fully staffed at this time. I have no need for another seamstress," she explained.

Just as Maggie's final hopes were dashed, a woman boldly walked up and stared at the dress in the box.

"This is exactly the kind of design I'm looking for. Come and see me tomorrow," the woman said. She gave Maggie her calling card and then abruptly left.

The card said: *Miss Minna Everleigh, 2131 South Dearborn Street.*

Maggie was overjoyed. She thanked Madame Bouvier and walked out with Mrs. Harmon and John.

"Thank ya so much for your help, Mrs. Harmon. I will always remember it," Maggie said sincerely.

"Margaret. I will always regret the position I put you in and am pleased to help you bridge your way to a professional life. You have an exquisite God-given talent, and it would be a shame to squander it," she said and left in her carriage.

Maggie was thrilled but curious about the mysterious woman, but she couldn't pass up a wonderful opportunity for a new custom client.

Mrs. Harmon kindly allowed Fiona to stay with Davey and Katie while Maggie visited Miss Everleigh.

The next day, Maggie took a streetcar to the address on the card.

The townhome was not as ornate as Harmon House or the Dakota; it was modestly appointed and consistent with other architecture in the city.

But as soon as the butler answered the door, she realized the inside of the home did not match the outside.

As she followed him through the foyer and hallway, her eyes widened, astonished at the big leafy palm trees in gold embossed planters, bright multi-colored rugs, wall-sized mirrors, gold-leaf wood on the walls, stairwell and shiny gold ceiling tiles.

But nothing could have prepared her for the opulence she saw. Not the fair, the Dakota, Donegal Hall, or Harmon House. This was in a class by itself.

When he opened the golden double doors to the oriental music room, she blinked her eyes a few times in surprise.

Maggie gasped in awe as she locked her gaze on the golden-clad room. In a way it reminded her of the Little Egypt sets at the fair with the curved pointed archways and intricate golden lanterns with tasseled bottoms.

She stood in the middle of the room, slowly circling to view every detail, from the overstuffed plush patterned sofas and chairs lining the walls to the solid gold-colored piano. The elaborate gold walls and ceilings, combined with the mirrors embedded in each curved arch around the room were shiny and nearly blinding.

"The room really knocks you off your feet, doesn't it?" Minna asked Maggie, appearing in the doorway. "I spared no expense for the best. The piano alone cost $15,000. As you can tell, I have a penchant for gold."

Stunned and speechless, Maggie just smiled awkwardly.

Minna Everleigh was well dressed and had pale milky skin, dark black frizzy hair and a thin pretty face. She was curiously unmarried for her thirties age, so Maggie imagined she was an unfortunate maiden heiress.

Given her overly embellished home and her style of dress, it was obvious she had impeccable but extreme and expensive tastes.

Minna sat down and motioned for Maggie to join her. As she sunk down into a stuffed chair, Minna served her tea from an all-gold tea service.

"I like what I saw from your work. Your clothes are intricate and detailed. And you obviously have a unique eye. I wear only silks and satins decorated with beads and pearls. As for the styles, I want new, I want different and I want to be the best-dressed woman in Chicago. My gentleman patrons expect the best in all they see here. And I don't care about those snooty over-plucked society matrons, but I'd love them to be flabbergasted when they see me on the street," she said with a slightly slanted grin.

"I would love to design your clothes, and I want to be honest from the start. I have two children at home, so I would have to work there," Maggie said firmly, not knowing if her statement would end the meeting.

Minna laughed. "I suppose someone has to have children or the world would eventually cease to exist. Fine. I can have the fabrics delivered to your home and have the final garments delivered to me. Now, let's talk design. I'll pay you $70 for a gown to start."

Maggie listened and wrote down everything Minna told her. Minna was fearless and welcomed unbridled innovation. She was the kind of client she always wished for—someone with whom she could push boundaries and invent something spectacular.

After an hour, Maggie's head was gleefully swirling with ideas.

"When will ya be wanting the clothes? I'm hand sewing, so I just need a schedule," Maggie said.

"Well, that won't do. I'll send a sewing machine over. I want your best work and I want it fast," Minna said.

Maggie smiled and thanked her, leaving her address on the table as Minna called for the butler to usher her out.

Suzanne Rudd Hamilton

With a spring in her step, Maggie promenaded to the streetcar like she was gliding on a cloud. It was her dream job.

As she got on the streetcar, she noticed a woman looked at her strangely, sneering and turning her head away. And when she went to sit down, another woman moved to another seat to avoid sitting next to her.

Maggie looked around at the other passengers, distraught and confused, until one older woman spat in her direction and said, "We don't consort with any brazen beet-haired floozies from the red-light district."

Utterly bewildered, Maggie put her head down and thought about what they said. Harlots often applied chemicals to their hair to create intense shades, but her hair was natural. And the woman had said "red-light district." As she was unfamiliar with that part of town, Maggie thought they must have been referring to the area near the townhome.

Confused after the uncomfortable streetcar ride, she strode back to her apartment deep in thought. Why would a rich woman with a palace of a home live in an area with houses of ill-repute? Then she remembered something Minna said—her gentleman patrons. All of a sudden it clicked. Minna and her house were one of those establishments.

By the time she reached home, she was embarrassed at her innocent ignorance and even more skeptical about working for such a person, so she didn't say anything to Fiona when she arrived home. She thanked her and promised her and Mrs. Donnelly a new shirt to repay their kindnesses.

The rest of the day, Maggie's mind wrestled back and forth about the job. No one would know who she was working for; she would only have to have to meet with Minna once in a while to plan new designs. She could work during the day and carefully hide the sewing machine and fabrics in from Mac. And she would get a sewing machine again and $70 per gown. That money would ease many of their financial woes and help save a little for a bigger apartment in the future.

But working for a madame bore heavy on her soul. After all she saw with men treating women poorly, could she work for Minna? She spent a sleepless night tossing and turning with her conscience.

By the next day, bolts of silk and satin fabrics arrived at the door with a brand-new sewing machine. It was shiny and beautiful—and after having two taken away, she really wanted it—so she reasoned Minna was a woman and she was in charge of everything and everyone, so that was progress. And she was just making clothes for a lady who paid handsomely, no matter what she did. She was all in.

A week later, the gown was delivered to Minna. The next day, a note came back with cash.

M –

Suzanne Rudd Hamilton

Fabulous. Here are my next instructions. And make something for my sister Ada too. I will send more fabrics and supplies.

M.E.

She made one dress for Minna and her sister and they were hooked. They sent materials and notes via messenger and had the finished clothes brought back to them. Once a month, Maggie would steal away for an hour and sit with Miss Minna at her home and plan new designs.

Maggie felt bad for deceiving Mac, but she was so inspired and fulfilled by the work. She hid the garments and sewing machine in the laundry bin and concealed tins all over the house with cash. She used a little here and there for groceries and items for the children, making sure not to buy anything extravagant or that would attract attention.

This went on nearly a year and Maggie was accumulating quite a nest egg while keeping her secret.

One day, she was visiting Minna and Ada to design some elaborate gowns they needed right away and just this once deliver a few clothing pieces she made for them. It was later in the afternoon than she usually arrived, but she needed to wait until Mrs. Donnelly could take time off.

At one point, the butler interrupted them with a distressed face and Minna and Ada left her alone in the room.

Suddenly, Maggie heard raised men's voices and Minna shouting at them. Then she heard sharp whistles and screaming, along with what sounded like hundreds of footsteps stamping about.

She froze in fear, silently hiding balled up in a corner of the room behind some furniture. She couldn't see what was going on and was afraid to know.

Someone burst through the door and looked around. It was a policeman. Terrified, she held her breath to escape notice and silently prayed. Soon he left the room.

For another hour, she kept still as a statue, not moving until long after she heard no noise remaining. She ventured out and peeked through the door. She heard nothing—and no one. The house was empty with an uneasy stillness.

Creeping outside the back door in the darkness, Maggie quickly walked to the streetcar stop. When she saw the time on a building's clock, she was worried. It was late and Mac would be home, wondering where she was.

She was rattled to her core. The police obviously took everyone away and had she been less lucky, she would have joined them in jail. Not understanding what really happened or why made no difference. Now she knew no money or professional satisfaction would repay the horror she experienced. She would never go back.

But there would be a price to pay at home. Mrs. Donnelly would have told him that she was meeting with a lady, so he didn't worry. And Mac would expect an explanation for her deception.

When she walked in the door, Mrs. Donnelly was gone and Mac was waiting there, playing with the children.

"Mrs. Donnelly was kind enough to make our meal. Let's eat it," he said in a stone-cold voice.

Maggie never heard him talk that way in the years they'd been married.

After they ate, she put the children to bed and went into the sitting room.

Mac was smoking his pipe on the sofa. She usually loved the aroma of his pipe, happily inhaling the smoke as she cuddled next to him.

This was different. His breathing was labored, and his usually warm eyes were steely with anger and disappointment.

Her heart saddened as she sat up straight next to him, ready to take her punishment. They couldn't speak loudly or they would wake the sleeping babes, but she understood his anger despite his hushed tones.

"Mrs. Donnelly told me yer were meeting someone. I want to know where yer were. I'm only asking once and I want the truth," he seethed.

Maggie got up and retrieved a metal tin from the cabinet and handed it to him.

"I've been making money," she said and opened the tin to reveal the cash. "I made garments for a few ladies to get some extra money, but I'm humiliated and ashamed to keep it from ya."

Mac's normally warm blue eyes fired to rage and his face reddened.

"I told you. I'm the head of this house and yer the mother of me wee bairn. I make the money and yer care for the house and children," he said, breathing heavier.

She knew lying to him was wrong, but his outrage struck a chord with her and her green eyes glowed with ire. She got up, went to the door and motioned for him to follow her.

Angered, she heeded her mother's advice, closed her eyes, breathed and counted to three. But after three, she was still mad.

"I am your wife and the mother of your children, but ya knew when ya married me, I want more in life than just that. I love to sew and make clothes. It's part of me and taking that away is like cutting off me arm. Ya work hard and I will say Hail Marys for the rest of me days for lying to you. That was wrong. But working hard to help me family is no crime that I know of and I'll not be apologizing for loving our family just as much as you," she said defiantly.

Mac stared at her for several minutes and silently puffed on his pipe, engulfing them in swirls of smoke.

"Aye, I understand yer," he said. He gently took her hand and led her back into the apartment and sat on the sofa.

She joined him and he put his arm around her. She pulled out a book and began to read. That was enough said about that.

She didn't need to tell Mac about the police or who she was working for. Maggie felt it was better left unsaid. They had an understanding now and would build on that.

The next day, a messenger came to the door with a note from Minna.

M-

Sorry for the raucous. It happens. I'm glad you made it home.

M.E.

Maggie asked the man to wait to deliver a reply and scrawled a quick note to Minna.

Miss Minna,

I regret that I will no longer be able to design and make your garments. I have enjoyed our relationship immensely and thank you for the opportunity, but for family reasons, I can no longer do the job.

Please have someone pick up the final completed dress, remaining supplies, fabrics, and the sewing machine.

Yours, Maggie

At the end of the week, a messenger arrived to pick up the dress and remaining fabrics, but didn't take the sewing machine.

"Ya forgot the machine," Maggie told him.

"No, ma'am," he said as he left and handed her a note and an envelope with money and a note in it.

M –

I understand but am sorry to lose you. I am now the best-dressed woman in Chicago because of you. I will never forget it. Please keep the sewing machine as a token of my admiration and esteem. I hope we will meet again.

M.E.

Maggie was speechless. Finally, she had a sewing machine of her own that no one could take away.

Suzanne Rudd Hamilton

Chapter Twenty-Two

Several months after she stopped working for Minna, Maggie was itching to try something else. Since she had a taste of success, she was ready for the next level, but puzzled as to what that was.

And now that Mac accepted her need to work, their relationship was thriving. They acted like honeymooners again. He brought her flowers sometimes and doted on her and the children at every opportunity, planning family outings and picnics.

And their love life was more vigorous. Despite sharing a bedroom with their children, they found little nooks and crannies anywhere to make love.

One night while sitting on the sofa reading, Mac blew out the candles, then mysteriously took her hand and led her to the fireplace. He laid a quilt down and slowly pulled her down on her knees with him. He gracefully took her hair down from its bun, tenderly combing it with his fingers until it cascaded down past her shoulders.

Then he touched her cheeks, stroking his finger down to her dress, unbuttoning it one at a time.

Maggie smiled, intrigued and excited by his bold effort. She sweetly kissed him on the neck while he unbuttoned the rest of her dress. As the dress fell, she discarded it to the side then removed her underdress and knelt there with the amber glow of the fireplace reflecting her bare skin.

Mac smiled and jumped up quickly to disrobe and then knelt in front of her, both staring at each other for a moment, then falling together in a passionate, unending kiss.

They made love in front of the soft, warm fire and fell asleep in each other's arms under the comfy quilt.

The next night, Mac came home with a skip in his step and a bouquet of daisies for Maggie.

He kissed her full on the lips and kissed Davey and Katie on their heads.

"Hello, me wife and me wee bairn. I have news," he said with his bright gleaming eyes dancing. "My boss is opening a brickyard just outside the city and asked me to manage it. And he will give me a raise and an allowance for a fine house near the brickyard. This weekend we can look around."

Maggie was thrilled. She wasn't sure about moving out of the city, away from Mrs. Donnelly, Fiona and her church, but the idea of her own home with her own grass for the children to run and play on was overwhelmingly appealing.

They took the train just outside the city. Maggie watched out the window, remembering her first train ride into Chicago. As if it were happening in reverse, gradually they left the brick buildings and smoke staked factories of the city and saw fields and grass abound.

They stopped at a small train station called Stony Creek. Maggie looked at the tiny train house in the vast green prairie and smiled.

Ambling along around the main street, Maggie noticed the makings of small town with a general store, barbershop, bank, tavern and livery, and a schoolhouse/church.

Past the main street within eyeshot, there were vast rolling hills and fields of grass interspersed with farms of corn, wheat and beans, surrounded by sprawling acreage and big oak trees.

Maggie grinned as she watched children romping and playing in the fields and in the streets.

She smiled and breathed in the smells of the crisp, clean air and the fields.

"Do yer like it?" Mac asked.

"Yes," she nodded with one tear streaming from the side of her eye. "It reminds me of home."

They walked to an office adjacent to the bank and Maggie paused before she went in. She noticed a sign next door that said *Store Available*.

They went to the office and met with the agent. As he went over the available homes, Maggie couldn't take her mind off the storefront.

The agent took them in his carriage and showed them several nice homes with two bedrooms, a sitting room and a separate kitchen with big backyards where they could plant a vegetable garden. They seemed ideal.

Maggie watched lovingly as she stood on the front porch of a home, while Mac chased Davey and Katie around. But she couldn't shake the visions of that storefront in her head.

"That store next to your office. Is it for sale or rent?" she asked the agent.

"Well, the owner left town and asked me to take care of it. Why do you ask?" he said.

"Tell me this—does it have a home above?" she asked.

"Yes, it does; it's somewhat smaller than these homes, but it has two bedrooms," he said.

Maggie's eyes sparkled. Her wheels began to turn on the carriage ride back with different scenarios spinning through her mind.

When they arrived at the estate office, she turned to Mac and blurted out, "I know this is not what we planned, but could we look at that storefront next door?" she asked excitedly.

"A storefront?" he said, puzzled.

"I was thinking. If it worked, I could have a tailoring shop and we could live above it. It has an apartment," she told him with excitement in her eyes.

Mac could see she was enthusiastic about the idea but was unsure.

"I guess there's no harm in looking," he said. She threw her arms around his neck and kissed him in delight.

"Please could we see the store now?" Maggie asked the agent. He shrugged his shoulders and went into the office to get the keys.

Maggie stood outside peering through the store window as her imagination went wild.

When the agent opened the door, she felt a whole world open up to her. Maggie could barely contain her glee with each step around the shop.

In the front, there was a counter and an open window display. She pictured dress forms with her clothes on them and a sign in the window offering custom dressmaking and tailoring. She saw a full size mirror where customers could admire themselves in her designs.

There was an open room in the back where she could sew, while her children played. In the corner, she visualized hanging privacy curtains for her clients to use when she fit their clothes.

Mac beamed as he watched his bride prance around the room, explaining every detail she had in mind.

His heart filled with happiness and love at her joy. He never saw her so happy.

Stairs led up to an apartment with a sitting room open to a full kitchen and two bedrooms.

Maggie's face drooped in disappointment when she saw the apartment. It was larger than their apartment now, but smaller than the homes they saw in the country.

As she stared at her children's angelic faces, she remembered their laughter as they ran around in the yard of the house they saw earlier and started to feel selfish.

"This won't do. Let's get the house with the yard," she sighed and slowly walked down the stairs, holding the children's hands.

On the train ride back to the city, while watching her read to their children, Mac saw the light dim from her eyes. He knew how much making clothes meant to her and it saddened his heart to see her dreams dashed.

After they put their tired children to bed, he kissed her and lovingly caressed her cheeks. Tears ran down her face.

"Me Maggie, it pains me to see the hurt in yer beautiful eyes. Yer the best mother and wife in the world, but there has to be something for ya too." He looked at her with his earnest sapphire eyes gleaming with love.

Maggie lay awake all night, wide-eyed with her mind whirling with ideas and possibilities. They could use the money she saved and the housing allowance to start slow. She could make pieces for some people or whole garments. And maybe sell fabrics and supplies, as many people made their own clothes. And she could offer tailoring for those who needed it. If she could get the special mercerized thread sent from Ireland, she could make Irish lace doilies and tablecloths.

But then doubtful and guilty thoughts crept in. What if there wasn't enough business? Many of the rich ladies still lived in the city. What if everyone there made their own clothes? Was she being selfish? Would her children be better off in a home with a yard and vegetable garden? Would they be cooped up in a small apartment forever? Is that what a good mother would do?

As uncertainty and disbelief flooded her senses, she began to feel ill. She ran over to the chamber pot and vomited.

"Are yer all right there, me dear?" Mac asked, groggily waking up.

Maggie shrugged it off as nervous butterflies in her stomach, but as she prepared breakfast later, she began to get nauseated at every smell in the kitchen.

Later, when the children were napping, she found herself weepy while mending clothes and put it all together in her mind. She was in the family way again.

Then the bell rang. It was the post and there was a letter from New York. It was from Caroline.

Suzanne Rudd Hamilton

Dear Maggie,

I wanted to write to let you know that Bryne unexpectedly passed a few months ago. I can tell only you that I didn't grieve for him. That dashing young man who swept me off my feet was long gone and replaced with a man who used me when he wanted and ignored me when he didn't.

I'm sorry to say you were right about everything. I knew it; I just didn't want to admit it. What I did to you was unforgivable. He could never satisfy his salacious appetite. And it killed him.

We told people he had a heart ailment, but he really died from a lowly unspeakable disease from one of those places he frequented.

Taking stock of my life, the children are off in school and I am alone. Really alone for the first time. I'm lost. I need my friend. I don't know if you're still my friend. I don't deserve a friend like you, but if you feel any kindness in your heart for me and have charity in your soul, I hope you will write me.

Wish, wish, shining star, make us be who we are, and if ye take us far from ours, keep us forever Anam Cara.

Your friend, Carrie

So many thoughts were bubbling up in Maggie's head. A new home, new baby, what to do about the store and now this. She laid down ill with overload and exhaustion and fell to sleep.

The children awakened her an hour later, asking for a snack.

Dazed, she got up and gave them some milk and shortbread cookies. She made a batch of for Mac to soften the news about another mouth to feed.

Mac was as surprised as Maggie when she told him. They loved their children and meant to have more, but the timing was awkward for their move, his new job and her daring venture.

"Let's just get the house with the big yard and the porch," she said. "I can't put this family into an apartment again with another on the way. I need to think of them and you."

Mac leaned over, kissed her cheek and hugged her tightly.

"Maggie my dear, I've never seen yer happier than when ya were standing in that shop dreaming of what could be. It's what yer want. Yer should have it. I'm putting me foot down," he said sweetly and kissed her.

"How can I start a business and have a new babe?" she asked and began to cry.

"Again with the waterfalls," he laughed. He dried her tears with a handkerchief. "The Maggie I know will find a way. Besides, I already wrote the agent and made the deal to rent the store and apartment."

Suzanne Rudd Hamilton

Maggie looked at him through her teary eyes and hugged him tightly.

Chapter Twenty-Three

The next Sunday, Maggie invited Mrs. Donnelly and Fiona to the apartment after church to share the good news about the move and the new baby and to say goodbye. As their new home was a train ride away, she knew she wouldn't see them very often.

They all wept and hugged each other. They promised to visit her on their day off, but she knew between church and the train ride there and back, their good intentions would likely go unfulfilled.

After they left, she felt a little empty. Although she gained something with every move, she seemed to always lose some of the little family she had.

For now, she held onto the hope that they would visit. Then she thought of Caroline. Should she write her? Should she forgive her?

She was glad Carrie realized who Bryne was and did not shed a tear or feel sorrow for his death. But as a God-fearing Catholic, Maggie said a prayer for his soul, knowing it would probably do no good.

Deciding it was only polite to answer the letter, she wrote to her.

Suzanne Rudd Hamilton

Dear Carrie,

I can't say I'm sorry to hear about Bryne, but I am sorry for your troubles. Loneliness can be a difficult burden to bear. I only hope you find a path that suits you and heals your heart.

Remember, me mother used to say, may today be better than yesterday, but not as good as tomorrow.

I wish you love and peace.

Your Maggie

Maggie didn't feel ready to tell her anything about her life, now if ever. She wasn't sure she could completely forgive and forget, but she was willing to walk on the road carefully on her terms and see where it took them.

"As me mother used to say, may the hinges of friendship never grow rusty," Maggie said to herself as she put the letter in the envelope.

A few weeks later, the McIntyre move was complete and they joined the other two hundred or so residents of their new town.

Amid the harried preparations and move, Maggie managed to sew Mac a smart new suit for his management debut at the brickyard.

Although he resisted donning the restrictive garb, as he said he wanted to be a working manager, among the men, Maggie convinced him that he needed to dress the part, at least at first.

Mac hated suits, so she tried to strike a balance between something well-tailored to fit his hard work-chiseled physique and comfort. The shoulders had a lot of space and the collar was softer, with a ribbon bow tie instead of a stiff one.

"I still hate these straightjackets, but I guess this one is a little better," Mac gruffed as he pulled at the suit from discomfort.

"Ya need to look like the boss, so you'll not be getting it dirty. Now go on with ya." She smiled and kissed him goodbye.

After they settled into the apartment, Maggie worked tirelessly setting up the shop. She placed a few dress forms in the window with some of the clothes she made for herself, including her traveling suit and her day frock with her signature herringbone vest, plus a church dress she made.

Mac made her a sign from wood and painted it to say, custom tailoring and dressmaking, just like the one she imagined the first time she saw the store.

With the shop set up and the kids in their playroom, Maggie waited and waited for people to come in. She watched a few women walk by for the first few days and curiously peer in, but no one entered.

She decided she needed more clothes in the window to tempt someone to come in, so she replicated some of her favorite pieces from her work for Mrs. Harmon, Minna and Fatima. Most of Fatima's costumes were not suitable for everyday women, but the experience made her expertly adept with scarves, which she wanted to introduce as a trend in women's clothing—something to wear around the neck, the head and even at the waist as a belt or as a skirt accent.

She dressed the window display with flowers in vases and colorful scarves to set a beautiful backdrop. Mac strung up a clothesline for her in the front window to show the beautiful pieces she just made to compliment the full-length outfits on the dress forms. Still, no one came in.

Feeling sick to her stomach from her condition and her perceived failure, she sat alone at the counter, sulking and defeated.

"What's the matter with me wonderful and talented missus?" Mac asked, smiling and handing her a bunch of wildflowers he picked on the way home.

Maggie kissed him for his kindness, but then took one whiff and felt nauseated.

"This baby seems to hate the smell of everything and no one has come into the store no matter what I do. No one. This was a mistake. Maybe there aren't enough women in this town to succeed," Maggie said with her head sunk low.

"It takes time for anything to get a foothold." He kissed her on the forehead and held her head on his chest, stroking her hair. "Me father used to say success is about getting up just one more time than yer fall."

Maggie sighed deeply and drifted into a daze. She loved when he stroked her hair. She felt loved and pampered and it gave her a sparkly tingling feeling.

"I'll tell yer one thing; your suit was a hit with me boss and some of the other men. I thought it must be me wedding day with all the compliments I received," he boasted.

She raised her head to gaze upon her newest design and noticed a big gash in a seam, a rip in the vest and a pulled thread.

"Now, Mr. David McIntyre, how did ya tear your suit? Were ya running around in the mud pretending to be a pig?" she scolded playfully and laughed.

Mac smiled at her and shrugged his shoulders.

"Take it off and I'll mend it. I'll tell ya, this is why ya can't have nice clothes," she laughed.

The next day, he reverted to a new pair of dungaree slacks, vest with a collared shirt and a tied scarf neckerchief she made for him.

She took a dress off one of the dress forms in the window and put his suit on it to repair and then heard Katie cry, so she went into the back.

When she returned, she was startled by a woman in the store, looking at the suit in the window.

Maggie grinned, excited at the first sign of life in her store and welcomed her.

"I would be pleased to help you, ma'am," Maggie said.

"Oh hello, I was just admiring this suit. I'm Mrs. Pickard, the reverend's wife, and I love the unique cut of this suit. My husband wears suits every day and hates everything I buy for him from the mail order," she said.

"Happy to meet you, Mrs. Pickard. I'm Mrs. McIntyre. My husband always picks and pulls at suits, so I designed this suit to give him breathing room," Maggie told her.

"That's my Robert too," she laughed. "Can you make him a suit like this?"

Maggie's eyes sparkled as she discussed every intricacy of the suit with her from the pattern to the style and fabric to the design and the fit.

After Mrs. Pickard left, she twirled around the store in glee, until she got dizzy.

She never considered men's clothing before, but men wear clothes too and good tailoring wasn't possible with mail order.

When Mac came home that evening, she was giddy with excitement.

"I sold my first garment. A whole suit like yours to the protestant minister's wife," Maggie said with pride.

Mac happily kissed her and eagerly picked her up off the floor without thinking, then realized her condition and put her down gently.

"That's great, me girl. I told yer it just took time," Mac said. They danced around the store laughing and singing with Davey and Katie.

Maggie decided to create some new pieces for men, like a take on her herringbone vest, and showcase them in the window.

As the unofficial town crier, Mrs. Pickard spread the word about Maggie like wildfire and little by little, women came in to look for their husbands and themselves.

The scarf idea was a unique proposition that intrigued several women, so Maggie made a few of different sizes and wore them a different way every day. Scarves were a very economical and versatile way to accessorize and accentuate any garment with distinctive style. Soon women would come in just to see what she'd done with her scarf that day.

As a reminder to herself that business tides can always turn, Maggie hung a sign in the shop with one of her mother's favorite sayings.

Luck never gives. It only lends.

A few months later, baby Michael was born and a proud Mac handed out cigars to everyone in town and at the brickyard.

Maggie and Mac christened Michael in their new parish in the next town, as Mr. Pickard's protestant church was the only church in their town.

Many of their new friends, including the Pickards, attended Michael's service, showing showed how much they embraced Mac and Maggie. Mrs. Donnelly and Fiona even took the train from the city for this occasion.

Holding Michael up at the altar, Maggie felt a warm sense of community and love seeing everyone gathered to share their joy.

Overwhelmed with a full heart, that night Maggie wrote to Caroline for the first time in nearly a year.

Dear Carrie,

I haven't written in a while, but I'm telling you now, I forgive you. I've come to a point in my life where I am truly happy. I have a wonderful man who loves me as I am and three beautiful children. And I have a business that allows me to do what I love.

As I watch my children playing, I'm reminded of the wonderful childhood you and I had together. It's been a long time healing, but if you're wanting to write to me, I would like that. Anam Cara.

Yours, Maggie

Suzanne Rudd Hamilton

Chapter Twenty-Four

Winter 1932

Maggie sat there with little Davey reading the scraps from the attic box. She was in a daze.

There were newspaper clippings about the Everleigh Club. One about an unfortunate scandal involving Marshall Field Jr. in 1905. His mistress of his shot him at the club while meeting with one of the girls in a room and he died a few hours later, after being taken home in his carriage.

Maggie smiled thinking how take-charge Minna probably had a hand in getting him back home to keep up appearances.

The other clipping was about the club's closing in 1911. The clip called it the most famous and luxurious house of prostitution in the country.

Maggie remembered the opulence of Minna's home and how she admired Minna for building her empire in her own way.

The program and postcards from the fair made the Columbia Exposition come back to life, from the glitz and the glamour to the memories of the people she met.

Looking through the program, she reflected on everything she learned from all those people living a whole world away.

A picture advertisement from her tailor shop put a big grin on Maggie's face. She pictured all the designs she made and her customers. Katie and her family took over the shop. Just as she'd hope, the craft and the love of creation were once again successfully passed from mother to daughter.

At the bottom of the box was a death notice. It read: *The celebrated New York society matriarch, the Viscountess of Donegal, died in her Dakota home in New York after a prolonged illness.*

A tear came to Maggie's eyes as she thought of Carrie. For the last twenty years of her life, they corresponded regularly. She told Maggie of her society escapades and travel adventures. Maggie told her about her family and the shop.

They were short letters. Maggie never knew if too much time had passed or too much had happened, but they were on different planes of existence.

The friendship they shared as girls was a precious memory, lost in the green rolling fields of Ireland. It could never be regained.

Maggie was lost in thought when Davey brought her a small satin pillow, stained yellow by time. It was the pillow Maggie made for Moira and Liam in New York.

Caroline sent back to Maggie with a few other remembrances before her death.

"What's Anam Cara mean?" he asked, handing her the pillow.

Maggie took the pillow and smiled.

"In Ireland, it means someone who is a true friend will always be close to you," she smiled, touching the pillow.

"Now for you, Mr. Adventure. Ya got me telling tales of old and I forgot what I came here. Your ma and pa are here to take ya home. But soon another fair will be landing in Chicago and your grandpop and I will take ya there. The last fair was the grandest experience of me life and now it's time for ya to see one with ya own eyes."

Davey scampered down the attic stairs, nearly hitting Mac on his way down.

"That boy has the energy of a runaway fire engine," Mac laughed. "He's a credit to his Irish and Scottish roots and has the red hair and green eyes to prove it."

"He gets the red hair and green eyes from me. Your hair is orange. Well, it used to be orange," she teased.

"Didn't your mother say the older the fiddle, the sweeter the tune? And your red hair comes from a bottle now." He laughed and kissed her.

"Yer know, I think that boy should have his own name that suits his person. From now on, let's call him Red."

Years passed, as did Mac, with Maggie by his side. Then it was Maggie's turn. But before she left, she put together a wooden box with beautiful layette, the family's christening gown, the satin embroidered pillow and a black velvet box containing her emerald wedding ring with a note.

Darling Red,

I'm so pleased to see you grow into a handsome man, just like your grandpop and your pa. I was hoping to dance a jig at your wedding and lay my eyes upon your wee bairn, but that wasn't in the plan.

I leave you some of meself to pass onto your family, when the time is right. I'm pleased to think of your wee bairn being held up in the church, wearing this beautiful christening gown, made by his old Gran Maggie.

The rhyme on this pillow is one I used to say to your pa and you when you were young. It's from Ireland and I hope you'll tell it to your littlens to remember where their people come from.

And if it pleases you, I hope you'll give me ring to your bride. The day your grandpop gave it to me was the happiest day of me life. He loved me 'til he parted, and I love him always. Considering it has the emerald in it, I believe it's the luckiest charm ever created.

Suzanne Rudd Hamilton

Even a leprechaun couldn't craft more luck than a lifetime of true love. I hope it blesses you and yours.

When you were little, you loved to hear about Ireland. I hope I imparted all the wisdom of our people to you. But here's one more. As me mother used to say, those we love don't go away, they walk beside us every day, unseen, unheard, but always near; still loved, still missed and very dear. Death leaves a heartache no one can heal, but love leaves a memory no one can steal.

Your Gran, Maggie

Fall 1945

A very pregnant Suzy and Red stood in the attic reading the letter from Maggie. They carefully looked through the box of the christening gown, blankets and pillow.

"This was my indoor playground," Red said, pointing around the attic. "I'd make up adventures here with the old junk and Gran would encourage me."

"I wish I could have known her," Suzy said. "Looking at these wonderful things she made and reading her letter, I can tell she was very special."

"She was a grand gal. A real spitfire, but the kindest woman you'd ever meet," Red smiled.

"I know—if it's a girl, we'll name her Margaret, but maybe we could call her Peg," Suzy said.

"Gran would love it." Red smiled and kissed Suzy. "Thank you for that. I hope our little Peg has every bit of her Great-Gran Maggie in her, from the red hair and green eyes to the fiery personality. Of course, with her mother's beauty and sweet songbird voice."

"You can teach her all Maggie taught you. And as long as she's loved as much as you were, she can't help but fulfill the legacy of her namesake and make her proud," Suzy said.

Red took the wooden box and they walked down the attic stairs.

Summer 1969

Peg McIntyre walks up the attic stairs looking for an escape. As a small girl, the attic was a place to dream and pretend she was someone else.

When she was a little older, it was a refuge to play guitar and sing, out of her parent's earshot.

Now she knew she had to be someone else, not who her parents wanted her to be.

She finds some vintage clothing in wooden boxes, including an old straw hat and herringbone vest. She put on the hat and vest and stuffs the rest in her backpack, slinging her guitar across her back. She turned around to take one last look at her childhood retreat and walked down the stairs. She would never see it again.

Suzanne Rudd Hamilton

Book 3, The Summer of Love B0B3C1427Z is Available Now for Amazon Preorder at discount price

What's Next?
A Timeless American Historical Romance

It's the Summer of Love, 1969, and red-haired Peg McIntyre is the spitting image of her Great-Gran Maggie with the family green eyes and fiery temper.

Just before her twenty-fourth birthday, Peg escapes the family home in Chicago and her parents, Suzy and Red, for a life in search of freedom, music and bliss.

The inescapable future that society and her parents had in mind is not what she wants, so she follows a friend and a dream to New York, where she finds adventure, unexpected love, and one amazing concert that changed the world.

Subscribe to my newsletter at www.suzanneruddhamilton.com for exclusive news and sneak peeks on this and more books coming soon. I typically start sneak peeks about three months before publication and show cover reveals and 1st chapter reads.

Plus, I give a behind-the-scenes look at all my books, where I got the ideas the inspiration "between the pages" of each book.

Suzanne Rudd Hamilton

The Sailor's Know is a Celtic symbol which stands for unconditional love. The name was given to it as the ancient sailor's wives used these ornaments to remember their loved ones, while they were far away.

The Celtic double spiral symbolizes the duality of nature and external balance. Opposites like life and death, yin and yang, feminine with masculine, sun and moon, light and darkness and day and night are shown to complement each other with equal weight and importance.

About the Author

Thank you for reading this book. I like to tell stories about women with heart, hope and humor. Life is full of all three and you need to have each to thrive and survive, much like all the people in this book.

I encourage everyone to make their own path in life, no matter what age. I did, but it took a long time.

I spent my first career trying to find my bliss in journalism, public relations, real estate, and marketing. Now I'm enjoying my second career—writing. I write in many genres for all ages, but I always try to tell stories of everyday life experiences in a fun-filled read. Originally from Chicago, my husband and I, along with my computer, are happy transplants in the warm and gentle breezes of Southwest Florida.

Please let me know what you think with a review on Bookbub.com, Goodreads.com or Amazon.com at

Suzanne Rudd Hamilton

https://www.amazon.com/review/create-review?&asin=B09XLW168D. I value the opinions of my readers and will always strive to entertain and give you a good feeling after the last page is read.

Feel free to reach out to me on my social media channels and sign up for my newsletter to get weekly short stories, bonus materials, name and book cover reveals, contests, giveaways, exclusive sneak peeks and updates on new releases.

I love to hear from my readers. You can sign up and find out what I'm working on and get some behind-the-pages information at *www.suzanneruddhamilton.com*. You can also follow me on social media at:

 @suzanneruddhamilton

 @suzanneruddhamilton

 @suzruddhamilton

 Suzanne Rudd Hamilton, Author

 @suzanneruddhamilton

 @suzanneruddhamilton

My Other Works

Welcome to my world. I write cozy mysteries, women's fiction, historical romances, books for middle grades and young adults and children's illustrated books under a couple derivatives of my name, listed below. My books are clean and friendly for any audience. If you want to read more from me, here are my works. All novels are available in paperback and eBook on Amazon.com and Kindle and soon to be available as audiobooks through Amazon.com/Audible:

Historical Romance: Suzanne Rudd Hamilton

A Timeless American Historical Romance Series:

Book 1: The Sailor and the Songbird
Book 2: Irish Eyes

Women's Fiction: Suzanne Rudd Hamilton

The Little Shoppes Books Series:

Book 1: Cupcakes, etc.
Book 2: Butterfly Bridal Boutique (Jan 2023 release)

Cozy/Detective Mystery: Suzanne Rudd Hamilton

Secret Senior Sleuths Society Series:

Book 1: Puzzle at Peacock Perch
Book 2: Peril at Peacock Perch (Nov. 2022 release)

Suzanne Rudd Hamilton

***Beck's Rules Mysteries Series*:**

Book 1: Beck's Rules

Middle Grade/Young Adult: Suzanne Rudd

The Growing Up Girls Series:

Book 1: Diary of a 6th Grade "C" Cup
Book 2: The One and Only Skizitz
Book 3: Popularity (August 2022 release)

Children's Picture Books: Suzanne Rudd

How an Angel Gets Its Wings

I also write plays for the performing arts: *Hollywood Whodunnit*; *Death, Debauchery and Dinner*; *Dames are Dangerous*; *Puzzle at Peacock Perch; Sounds and Silence;* and the musical *Welcome Home*.

With Love and Appreciation

This book is dedicated to my family and friends who help me break down obstacles, jump over hurdles, and leap ahead—and who pick me up each time I get knocked down.

Thanks to my "Pens" and other writer friends and colleagues for your encouragement and direction.

And to my safety nets—editor Andie cover artist Elizabeth, and my ARC and beta readers—thanks for all your invaluable input and support.

To my readers, thanks for coming along on the ride.

Printed in Great Britain
by Amazon